WHALE MAIL

BUREAU OF MAGIC ABUSE

PATTY JANSEN

GET FREE EBOOKS

Visit pattyjansen.com
or scan the QR code below with your phone to get four series
starter ebooks for free!

CHAPTER 1

It was towards the end of the day and work was almost done when Perrin climbed the stairs to the top floor of the Bureau of Magic Abuse.

He wore his spiffy new uniform: black trousers and a crisp white shirt with a scarf with the council's emblem on it, a grey hat and a dark red trench coat.

It was a great uniform, even if he said so himself, and with his knowledge of fine clothing from his previous life, he had a hand in having it designed.

In one hand, he carried his cage with two magic sniffers, each in a separate compartment. Both animals were running backwards and forwards through the straw in the bottom of the cage. They were hungry. For the younger animal, Mika, one out of Perrin's own litter, this was the first trip on duty. For most of the day, Yaro, the older animal and Mika's father, had kept the youngster in check, but now both were too excited to hide in the straw and pretend nothing was happening.

As Perrin climbed the stairs, the animals both stood on their hind legs, front paws holding onto the bars of the cage, bushy tails bobbing as Perrin walked. Excited and very alert in a *where is my food?* kind of way.

At the top of the stairs, Perrin came out into the large room that held the rows of desks for the magic inspectors to take their notes and fill in their forms and report books at the end of the work day.

This room exhibited the usual state of organised afternoon chaos. Each desk belonged to an inspector. The desks stood in rows placed between book cases with their messy shelves overflowing with books and papers. Cages with magic sniffers stood everywhere. A couple of animals were hissing at each other through the bars of their cages while their owners caught up on events of the day.

Perrin hauled the cage with the magic sniffers in between the desks, greeting his colleagues along the way.

It had been a fairly normal day as far as things were normal in a magic inspector's life. Perrin had gone around the local inns and a couple of shops in town to check on their store rooms for illegal magic. He had chatted with the owners, whom he knew well by now. After starting in the job almost a year ago, he felt like he had settled in to his tasks.

He pulled the big book off the shelf and opened it at the page where he had left off the previous day, recording the discovery of a few magic items in a vegetable shop. He had warned the owner, and the owner had assured him that he would make repairs, dispose of the items and notify the supplier of those items of the discovery of illegal magic. Perrin had gone back to check today, and found that the offending items were packed in a box, ready to be shipped back to whatever magical realm they had come from.

The magic inspectors were keeping Tamba safe, because magic was not allowed here. Tamba was a place between the worlds where all types of magic worked, and allowing each and every one of them into town would be extremely dangerous.

But the magic inspectors were on top of things.

While Perrin started to write his report, someone walked past his desk, someone sounding puffed and bothered, someone wearing the red trenchcoat but brightly striped red and white stockings.

Perrin looked up. "Verbena!"

"Yes?"

She turned around. Her face was red from rushing. She always tended to be on the late side and therefore always had to hurry.

"What's with the socks?"

"These ones?" She lifted the hem of her coat, showing the offending bright, hand-knitted items for all to see. Several inspectors raised their eyebrows. "My sister made them for me."

"Didn't Inspector Carbin say that any clothing we can wear underneath our uniform has to be dignified and muted in colour?"

"Oh." Her cheeks grew even more red. "She got some red wool at the markets but it wasn't enough, so she made white stripes. I think it looks nice. Do you really think Inspector Carbin won't like them?"

"Well, I guess you'll have to wait what she says."

Perrin didn't think the inspector would like them, because brightly striped socks didn't fall under any definition of *dignified*, but he could also not get himself to say that. *He* quite liked them. It was something that his deceased flamboyant partner Atreyo would have liked, whose passing—three years ago—he'd commemorated last week, alone in his room with a candle on the windowsill.

Likely, Verbena's sister had bought white wool because it was cheaper, or because she had unpicked a garment she had either found or been given by one of her "patrons". And it was a wonder that, with seven children by seven different fathers, Verbena's sister had any time to knit at all.

Verbena grabbed a book off the shelf, and Perrin watched her brightly striped socks bob up and down as she walked to an empty desk.

At that moment, the receptionist from the public office downstairs came running up the stairs.

"There is a fight in the harbour," this man called out. His face looked red and flustered.

He was one of the administrative people who worked not directly for the inspectors, but to service all the Bureau of Magic Abuse's employees in the building. The public office was one of the recent additions to the Bureau's services. In the room downstairs, citizens could come to have items checked for magic free of charge, so that no one could complain that they didn't know that an object contained magic because they couldn't afford to pay any of the private operators who, half the time, were only interested in selling additional magical items in order to detect magic anyway.

"A fight?" Inspector Carbin said. "I presume the guards are dealing with it?" She was just coming out of her office, also about to go home, by the look of things. She looked around the office. Her gaze landed on Verbena's socks. Her eyebrows flicked up.

"Apparently, a magical device was used," the man said.

"What? In the middle of the city? That's a bit hard to believe."

"That's what he said. I believe he's a witness. He specifically asked for action from the Bureau," the man said.

"Is this person still here?" Inspector Carbin asked.

Perrin could almost hear her desire to roll her eyes in her voice. She was about to go home after all.

"I will tell him to come upstairs."

The man disappeared again.

Inspector Carbin pulled a face but went into her office.

She gestured for the inspectors to stay.

Great. Now Perrin was stuck here with a bunch of cranky and hungry magic sniffers. That was his punishment for doing his job properly and not getting out the door quickly enough.

The receptionist returned quickly with another man, who looked like a dock worker straight from the harbour front. He was huge and had hands as big as shovels. His face was broad, his hair messy, and he looked around the office as if he came into a magical realm.

He seemed star-struck.

"This is Bix. He works as a labourer in the harbour. He was inside the venue where the fight started."

The man looked around at the bookcases, the rows of desks, the work schedules pinned on the walls, with his mouth hanging open.

The receptionist prompted, "Now, Bix, tell the inspectors what you've seen and what you just said to me."

"Well," the man said and then he looked around the twenty-odd officers in uniform who were still in the room.

The receptionist reminded him: "Do tell us, because if it is true what you're saying, we need to act quickly."

"For some days now, we seen these strange characters in the harbour," the man said.

Inspector Carbin snorted. "Surely strange characters come into the harbour all the time. This wouldn't be the first time that something shady happens out there?"

Her voice trembled with sarcasm. Boy, she really did want to go home.

The man opened his mouth, but closed it again. He stared at her. For as much as such a huge man could be afraid of a slight, middle-aged woman, he looked afraid.

"My colleague is a little touchy today," the receptionist said to him. "But please tell us what you saw today."

The worker turned to the receptionist and continued, "They was strange characters, with masks over their faces. They was all covered up with long jackets and gloves and that. There was rumours they was whalers. Some said they was buying harpoons."

Inspector Carbin said, "As disgusting and illegal as that is, it's also the responsibility of the regular guards."

"Please forget about the embellishments of the story," the receptionist said to his charge. "I don't care who or what they were. Tell us what you saw."

"But it's important what they were. Because that's what got them into trouble. They was buying things they was not supposed to have and doing things they was not supposed to do. Even in the harbour. The city people may not think much of us, but we got standards."

"The story, please."

"Well, I went into *The Happy Sailor*, like we do mostly after work, and I notice this ruckus at the back of the room."

"Ruckus?"

"You know, a fight. People yelling at each other, with bad language. Real bad language. The owner, good old Pip, was trying to calm them down because he's the one that gets to pay for the broken windows and stuff."

"Who was fighting?"

"That was these strangers. And they got someone with his back against the wall. I didn't think much of it because it was only Duco and he is always getting himself into trouble, ripping people off and that. But then I noticed the others. And they was the strangers. Duco is a small time swindler, but he doesn't usually mess with the big guys. He doesn't mess with magic. But these guys, they was something different altogether. Wearing masks, covering up their entire bodies. They had yellow eyes, like a snake. One man takes out this device like a magical globe and then he put it against the throat of poor old Duco that him and his mates cornered. This magical glowing snake came out of the globe and it wound around the man's neck and forced him to speak. But what he said made no sense, and the words sounded like they came out of the depths of hell."

All the magic inspectors looked at each other, and worry flitted over one or two faces.

And then Inspector Carbin said, "A truth globe."

"I don't know. I didn't hear anyone tell me what it was. But it was scary. And Duco was so scared he wet his pants. Not that he often needs a lot of help doing that, much as he's half-pissed most the time."

Inspector Carbin continued, "Truth globes are highly dangerous, because they are rarely about the truth. That's what they will tell you, but they can be used to make people confess to things they never did just so that they can be punished."

"Yeah, that's what these people did. They were asking poor Duco if he had something they was looking for, and he said that he knew where it was, so they took him away. But none of us believed that. Duco has nothing. He knows nothing. If he ever gets anything, he sells it to pay his debts to other shady characters. And the stuff he gets involved in is nothing that people from the realms would send anyone with scary glowing globes to get. There was no way that this man would have known where this thing was."

"What was it they were asking for?"

He shrugged. "I don't know. It was noisy, I didn't hear and I don't know anything about stuff like that anyway."

"And they took him away just like that?"

"Well no, because that was how the fight started, because Duco, for all that he's shady, got some angry friends, and his brother was also watching. They started this fight, and then one of these strange masked characters pulls out another magical thing and starts blasting people with it. That's when I got scared and I came here."

"You mean that's happening still right now?"

"Still going on as I came here. The guards are there, but they can't do much. They was just watching outside. They said someone go to warn the Bureau, so I did. That's all."

A worried expression came over Inspector Carbin's face. The inspectors were used to dealing with magic used in kitchens of inns. They weren't set up as a magical fighting force, but if a magical item had come into the city already, they were the only ones who could do something about it.

"Let's go check it out," she said.

CHAPTER 2

The man seemed disappointed when Inspector Carbin said they needed to prepare and they'd check it out later. He'd probably expected to come running back to the fight with a knight in shining armour in tow, in the form of a group of magic inspectors.

After the man had left with the receptionist, Inspector Carbin gathered all the magic inspectors that were still in the upstairs room in her office. They were about ten in total, and this included Perrin and Verbena.

They all looked at each other.

"Guess we're the unlucky ones," said Regis. He was one of the inspectors who had been at the bureau for at least ten years and commanded great respect from his colleagues.

A few chuckled, uneasily.

"We need to sort out what's going on here," Inspector Carbin said, her voice grave, and she explained what the man had told her for those who hadn't heard the story.

When she finished, she said, "I appreciate that none of this is in your job description, but it is not in mine either. I don't think anyone in the council realised how quickly magic would seep into the city once they started encouraging people from the realms to visit. We've been caught sleepwalking. We thought we would have to deal with magic potions and other small stuff, but we're going to have to employ people with more serious magic skills."

This was already agreed by the council, in fact. It was just that finding those people who were also willing to work in Tamba was a challenge.

Come and work as magician for the purpose of stamping out magic was not a great job advertisement, since magicians derived their fame from magic and therefore had an interest in the continuation of magic.

Inspector Carbin sighed.

"But that doesn't help us right now. If there are people in town using serious magic, we are the town's only defense against it, unprepared as we are. I am asking for volunteers, but I am also going to suggest to you that your willingness to help will be looked upon kindly when the time comes for promotions and such."

She looked around, but no one dared speak up that they didn't want to come. They were very much in this together.

They all understood Tamba's precarious situation, and also if they did nothing, the next round of trouble would be worse.

Inspector Carbin continued, "But I'm also aware that there will be a risk to you, and therefore I'll authorise something we've never done: the use of magical items. We have a store of them in this building, and some will be very useful for protecting our staff members."

Yes, there were storage rooms downstairs that held confiscated items of magic.

"Before anyone says it, I will confess that the irony of using magic to combat illegal magic is not lost on me, but I guess the priority is that we all want to go home after we do a job like this."

There were no jokes or smart comments.

There had been a genuine change in the general atmosphere at the Bureau. The magic inspectors realised that theirs was more than just another job that anyone could do if you showed them how and paid them enough.

Being a magic inspector could be dangerous. Very dangerous.

Perrin followed the inspectors down the stairs.

The walls in the stairwell displayed images of the short but proud history of the Bureau.

It started with the creating of the agency, not even fifteen years ago, by Inspector Carbin, then of the Mayor's Department of Law. The formal declaration of the inception of the agency hung on the wall. The Bureau's moving into the building two years later. A commemorative plaque was a reminder of that event.

Various paintings depicted other historic scenes. The extension of the building to include a second floor. The arrival of cages of magic sniffers. A class on how to spot magic by a visiting Solanian grand wizard.

Over the more than ten years of its operation, inspectors had confiscated many magical items. Most were small things, like magic buttons that cast an illusion over a cotton shirt that made it look like silken brocade. Or magic sugar that made those who ate it want more.

The small items were usually destroyed, but the more substantial items were all still held in the building for lack of a better purpose for them. Very few of these items were ever claimed by their owners, since claiming an item required admitting illegal possession of that item. Most cross-border traders considered confiscated goods as a write-off.

The collections were held in storage rooms on the ground floor of the building.

In the past few months, some poor administrative clerk had gone through and catalogued all the items, and rather than haphazardly thrown in crates, they were stored in labelled boxes that said things like *magic shields*, and *invisibility devices* and *deception devices* and, most dangerously, *purpose unknown*.

All inspectors filed into the narrow space in between the storage racks.

Inspector Carbin explained how the items here were unique and often dangerous, but then she said, "Go ahead, pick something that you think you can use. I would suggest that you pick something that protects you rather than a device designed for attack. You will appreciate that we're not supposed to use these items, so keep it modest. Don't pick anything of which you're not sure what it does. I don't want the mayor to get upset with us. Try to run a quick test on whatever item you choose, in the hallway, please."

When she finished speaking, the inspectors all looked at each other like little kids being set free inside a candy shop. As if no one wanted to appear too keen to start looking for the coolest device to use.

"Well, I like the idea of a magic shield," Regis said, while he took a box off the shelf.

Inside lay a couple of cylinders made from a smooth, glass-like material, open on one end.

He picked one out and moved his finger to the button on the side—

"In the hallway," Inspector Carbin reminded him.

Perrin also grabbed a cylinder and followed Regis out of the room.

Regis pointed the cylinder at the empty corridor and pressed.

Something went *zoop*. An umbrella-like shield of light sprang out of the open end of the cylinder. It shimmered and vibrated.

"Now what do I do with this?" Regis asked. He turned around. The shield followed his movement.

A colleague, Hendon, stuck out his hand. It went straight through the shimmering shield. He laughed. "That tickles."

"What does it actually do?" Verbena asked.

Perrin took his tube and pressed the button as he approached Regis. The shield sprang up like an umbrella.

He swung his arms until the two shields collided.

A bright flash tore through the hallway. The cylinder flew out of Regis' hand. Regis himself flailed backwards, falling against the wall.

Perrin released the button and his shield disappeared. He held out a hand to help Regis to get back to his feet.

"You can have this," he said, and handed the cylinder to Verbena. "This seems an excellent device for protection."

"What about you?" she asked, eying the empty box.

"I'll find something else."

A squeal of hysterical laughter came from down the hallway.

Three other inspectors stood there. One held a device that spat out a spray of sparks that glittered so much that Perrin couldn't see who the inspectors were. The sparks fell to the ground in a waterfall of light that formed a puddle that surrounded the inspectors. One of them dipped the tip of his shoe into the shimmering puddle, and it dissolved.

The inspector who held the device copped most of the sparks in the face. As a result, the top half of his body disappeared. You could still somewhat see where it was because of a shimmering outline, but the rest of the body had become transparent.

It was kind of immature, a bunch of magic inspectors going through boxes of magic items like kids in a lolly shop. He wondered who had prodded Inspector Carbin in which places to allow this to happen. Magic inspection lay at this weird conjecture of needing to stop the magic and needing magic to detect the magic in order to stop it.

Perrin went back into the storeroom.

He reached into another box and pulled out a jade and silver amulet on a gold chain. He showed it to Verbena.

"What is it?" she asked.

"You use it like this."

He pressed the jade against her forehead.

She winced. "Ouch, that stings."

The jade in the pendant glowed with green.

"See?"

He held it up.

"What does that mean?"

"It means you're telling the truth."

"But you didn't ask me a question."

"Then tell me how many children your sister has." He put the amulet against her forehead again.

She responded without hesitating. "Seven—ouch!"

The stone now glowed a dull red.

"It says you're lying."

"I'm not. That thing is wrong. She has seven."

"There are none forthcoming that you don't know about?"

She opened her mouth, said nothing, and closed it again. "If that is true... I'll kill her. What does she think I am?"

Thinking it wise not to comment any further, Perrin hung the chain around his neck.

Verbena's face still looked disturbed.

All around them, inspectors were testing out different items.

Hendon had put on a hat that made half his face disappear. Another had found a pendant that let out a constant stream of sparks when someone touched it. But it didn't seem to have any effect.

In another box, Perrin found a metal staff that stung him when he put both his hands on it. He slid that in his pocket. He could prod someone with it in uncomfortable places.

He also found a tiny box of stink pills, an item he remembered from Atreyo. These were eggs of an insect that lived in the desert and that, when disturbed, gave out the most disgusting smell to drive off predators. They were said to last for about ten years, so Perrin opened the box a sliver to see if they still worked.

A puff of air came out.

In the bottom of the box lay about twenty of the oblong eggs, slightly floppy, blue-grey shapes the length of the nail on his little finger.

"Oy, what's that stink?" someone called out.

The other inspectors all ran into the hallway, cursing and gagging.

Perrin shut the box and put it in his pocket. He repressed a smile, remembering how Atreyo had once used these stink pills to get rid of a very insistent seller of cheap sweets who had accosted Perrin and Atreyo in a bar on their travels.

"I'm not going back in there," someone said in the hallway.

"We're just about done clowning anyway," Inspector Carbin said. "Let's go."

"Are you coming as well?" an inspector asked her.

"Yes. I know this might be dangerous. You weren't trained to do this—neither was I. We'll share the danger and the victories. I can't, in good faith, ask you to risk your lives to do something you're not properly trained to do and stay in my safe office myself."

When he first came to work for the Bureau, Perrin had often thought of Julianna Carbin as harsh and strict, but although she was those things, she also had a deep sense of duty for the agency she had been instrumental in creating.

CHAPTER 3

It was a strange and motley crew of inspectors that made its way out of the building not much later. No longer dressed in recognisable uniforms, they wore a collection of strange hats, dusty cloaks and strange-looking devices in back packs. Some carried staffs and one had a coil of magic rope over his shoulder. Inspector Carbin wore a pink fluffy hat with a string of pompoms dangling from it. The garment cast a magical illusion that made her look like an old witch with a hairy mole on her nose.

In the scheme of things, Verbena's brightly striped socks looked normal.

Dusk was falling in the city, and shop owners were closing up their businesses, ready to go home for the day. The last shoppers were carrying their purchases home.

Some of them gave the band of strangely dressed inspectors puzzled looks.

A little boy pointed and said, "Look there, wizards! Look at the ugly witch!"

His mother looked where he pointed, and a horrified expression came over her face.

"Be quiet, you. Those are magic inspectors. Don't talk about other people while they can hear it."

The kid's eyes went wide, and he continued to stare.

Several inspectors chuckled.

But they soon passed the town square and then went into the narrow streets of the harbour district. Serious expressions returned to the inspectors' faces. Despite the somewhat silly outfits, this was not a fun expedition.

If Perrin had hoped, in a secret, cowardly part of his mind, that the fight had stopped in the time that had passed between when the dockworker Bix had left the scene, walked through the streets and reported the goings on to the Bureau, he was sadly disappointed.

Yells and shouts and the sound of breaking glass echoed through the narrow street.

In the time since Bix had left, the disturbance had spread to the alley at the side of the inn, and had grown into an all-out brawl between people in various states of drunkenness.

In the chaos, it was very hard to see who was fighting whom or where to start investigating.

A single guard was standing on the corner of the alley, hopelessly outnumbered and not sure what to do.

Inspector Carbin went to speak to him.

"What's going on here?"

He gave her a startled look. "Uhm... madam?"

"Urgh." Inspector Carbin yanked off the pink hat and changed from the mole-faced witch into herself.

The guard's face cleared. "Oh, it's you."

"Yes, it's me, and I've brought a team. What's going on here?"

"I'm holding this position while my colleague is drumming up reinforcements."

"What's up with these louts?"

"My partner and I were walking past when we noticed unrest in the inn. We tried to stop them fighting, but we might as well have shouted at the wind to stop blowing."

Inspector Carbin asked, "Did you spot anything that indicates the use of magic?"

"We did, for a bit, but we couldn't get close enough to see where it was coming from. Honestly, it was far too crowded in that place."

"Did you establish who were fighting?"

"There are some strangers in town," he began to say, but at that moment a great shouting match broke out and the rest of his words were drowned out by the noise.

The mood in the crowd had changed.

Someone shouted, but it was not a burst of anger. It was a cry of fear.

People retreated. Several young men ran away, one covering his head with a jacket.

More and more people started running away. First those who had been close to the fight, and then others followed.

"Come on," Inspector Carbin said. She had put her pink hat back on and had changed back into a witch.

"What's happening?" Verbena asked Perrin.

"I don't know. Come on, let's stay together."

Inspector Carbin pushed ahead through the crowd.

Before convincing the council that a service that kept magic in check was necessary, she had been a city guard.

But Perrin was not a fighter and had no guard training, and neither did the others in the group.

He met the eyes of another inspector, whose face looked terrified.

Verbena made a dapper picture with her magic cylinder in

one hand and the baton, the only weapon that inspectors were legally allowed to carry, in the other.

Perrin hoped he appeared as brave as Verbena, but didn't think he succeeded. He slid his hand in his pocket and held onto the magic staff. It tickled his skin. Hopefully, he wouldn't have to use it, because he had no idea what it did other than make his skin prick. He followed Inspector Carbin. She held onto her pink hat with one hand, a serious look on her witchy face. Verbena walked behind him.

The crowd jostled around them. And what a range of people they were. Sailors, common townsfolk, ladies of ill repute, bandits, wizards and thieves, drunkards.

Most of them were trying to wrestle their way out of the narrow alley, while the inspectors went against the stream to go into it.

The resulting log jam took a while to clear.

The fight at the very back of the dead-end alley concentrated around a group of people who stood on the steps to the side entrance of one of the harbourside inns. This area, normally the place where establishments put out their rubbish bins, had become a battlefield. It was hard to see who or even how many people were involved.

Perrin recognised a few townsfolk, colourful characters known to law enforcement, on one side of the fight. But on the other side... as Bix had said, some of them were strange characters indeed. They wore dark masks over their faces with tiny holes for their eyes. The masks were made from stiff cloth and depicted creatures with long snouts. The fabric was black with intricate patterns in gold paint.

The rest of their bodies were also completely covered: they wore dark hats, long-sleeved shirts, gloves, leather trousers and tall boots.

They held a local man holed up against the wall of the building. Perrin had seen this old fellow in the harbour before, although he wasn't familiar with what he did. Shady business, probably.

He stood against the wall, facing three masked men, holding his hands up. His face was red. One attacker held a knife.

Inspector Carbin yelled, "Hey, you, stop immediately!"

The strangers all turned around at once. There were five of them, all dressed in black and wearing similar kinds of masks.

Perrin could see the eyes of one: dark orange irises with a slitted pupil. Definitely not humans.

"Thank the heavens, Inspector," the old man who had been the victim said. "I told these miscreants that someone had gone to warn you."

"You're the man known as Duco?"

"I am, Madam."

"What was going on between you?" Inspector Carbin asked.

"They accused me of stealing something. I don't even know what sort of thing they were talking about. I told them they had the wrong man."

"What about you?" Inspector Carbin asked of one of the attackers. This was a tall fellow, clad in black from head to foot. A thin slit between layers of fabric showed two glinting green eyes with slitted pupils.

"Careful," Perrin said in a low voice.

Duco took the opportunity to scurry between the inspectors to safety.

"I'm asking you a question," Inspector Carbin said, her voice loud and clear. "It's your right to refuse to answer, but not answering may lead to your arrest, in which case you'll have to come before the court and answer under oath before a judge. I leave the choice up to you."

The attackers remained silent. Besides the green-eyed character, there was another with orange eyes and a much shorter one with dark eyes and two others who hid behind rubbish bins.

Inspector Carbin repeated, "Again, I'm asking a question. It will be beneficial to you if you answer it. Who are you and why did you threaten this old man? What are you looking for?"

After another moment of deep silence, one of the strangers whistled.

The figure facing Inspector Carbin backed away.

Then the one with the orange eyes slunk in between the rubbish bins.

"All right, I've had enough. Arrest them!" Inspector Carbin yelled.

The team sprang into action.

The wall that closed the end of the alley was taller than a person, but one of the strangers ran a few steps and jumped to the top, as if it was knee high.

"Did you see that?" someone yelled.

But even if people hadn't seen it, the other four strangers followed their comrade's example, and all jumped on top of the wall with ease.

Inspector Carbin called out, "Arrest them. They're trespassing on private land."

One inspector gave a colleague a leg up, but this was awkward because the man in question had chosen an illusion cape as magical aid and that got caught between his knees and the wall. Because it was an illusion cape, he couldn't see it, so he stood there with his hands flailing. He made it to the top because of his colleague's pushing, albeit rather unceremoniously and with some swearing.

Meanwhile, the strangers ran nimbly along the top of the wall to the inn's side. The inn also offered accommodation, and the back of the building was three floors tall.

But the sheer wall with small windows did not deter the

attackers. The first one clambered up, holding onto the down-pipe, all the way to the roof.

A young man in the crowd of onlookers yelled, "Look, look!"

Up on the roof of the inn sat another creature of similar human-like build, but without the face covering. It looked, for want of a better word, like a giant human sized cat wearing clothes.

The last of the five were now climbing up the drainpipe.

Perrin searched his pockets, but had brought nothing useful for a situation like this.

Someone behind him yelled, "Let me through!"

It was another inspector, with the magic rope from the store of confiscated items. In the space hastily vacated by curious citizens, he swung it and threw it into the air. The rope shivered. It formed a loop which fell over the last cat-man still climbing the drainpipe.

An inspector grabbed the end, and together they pulled and pulled. For a moment it looked like the cat-man might have to let go, but then a flash of blue fire lept from his fingers. It travelled along the rope for a short distance, and then the rope slid off him in two parts and fell to the ground, the ends smoking. He reached the roof safely.

The attackers ran over the roof of the inn to the back of the building, where they jumped across another alley and vanished.

Perrin followed the inspectors in running around the block, but by the time they got to the alley, the attackers were long gone.

Well, damn.

"What did these characters want?" Inspector Carbin asked.

She had taken off the pink hat and was panting. She looked more dishevelled than Perrin had ever seen her.

"They were looking for something," the city guard said. "They came into the inn accusing people of having stolen or hiding stuff. The citizens took offense to that. There are many things we are in Tamba, but thieves, we are not."

"Who did they speak to?"

"Random people, it seems. None of the usual suspects. We're working on a list of names."

"I'd be interested in a copy. If they appear again, please call us sooner."

CHAPTER 4

The inspectors walked back to the Bureau in a bedraggled group, carrying their useless magical items. Perrin felt as exhausted as Inspector Carbin had looked.

No one said it out loud, but it became ever more obvious that in order to fight magic, the Bureau would have to employ more serious measures than just a bunch of rat-like creatures with an ability to detect petty magic in inn kitchens. And even the use of confiscated magical items—illegally—made little sense unless the inspectors knew how to use them.

Talking about magic sniffers, he'd left his animals in the office, so he needed to pick them up first. They were even more cranky and hungry than they had been before.

Perrin lugged the cage through the town.

He wasn't used to running through the streets anymore, and none of the active guard work, like chasing or arresting people, clambering over fences or up ladders, had ever come naturally to him, anyway.

He made his way through the dark streets, where all the

shops were already closed and people had gone home. The sound of voices drifted out of the windows of houses, where people were sitting around after dinner, talking and laughing. The warm glow of light radiated from the windows.

To his surprise, Dorella was still in the tea shop where Perrin lived on the top floor. She was sitting at a table in the corner with several books spread over the table.

"You're late," she said without looking up.

"Yes, we had a bit of a problem and needed to chase some characters down in the harbour district."

Now she looked up and let her gaze roam over his dishevelled and scuffed clothing.

"Oh, poor you. I have some tea. Would you like some?"

"I would never say no to that. But I need to feed these guys first." He held up the cage where both creatures were running along the bars of the cage, raising themselves on their hind legs when they got to the corner and then turning around and running back the other way.

"I'll wait." She went back to her books.

Perrin stumbled up the stairs to the apartment where he had lived since his partner Atreyo's unfortunate death. With the money wrangled from Atreyo's rich family, he'd been able to buy the rooms.

The two magic sniffers squeaked and the other animals in the cages in his room also squeaked. He had eight of the creatures, soon to be more, but Frida was still in one piece, even if her belly stuck out so much that he wondered how many young she carried.

He transferred both magic sniffers to their own cages and shook the grain out of the bag into their trays. The excited squeaking made place for the crunching and nibbling of sharp teeth, chewing dry grain. He'd come back to give them fruit later.

Perrin went back to the shop and sank down at the table, as Dorella closed her books and put them in a stack.

"Doing the monthly figures?" he said while she walked to the kitchen.

"Yes, it's such a joy to do this every month."

He could hear her rolling her eyes while she said that. She came back to the counter carrying a teapot, and she grabbed some cups from the cupboard containing the tableware she would use to serve her customers. She poured steaming, dark tea.

"I shouldn't complain, though. The shop has been doing quite well recently."

She set the cups on a tray and carried it to the table and sat down with Perrin. The wonderful aromatic smell drifted on the air.

Perrin picked up his tea, stirred in some cream and drank in silence.

Dorella had also brought a plate of biscuits. There were always quite a few leftovers from the day's trading, and those biscuits she would sometimes give to people who came to collect donations for the poorhouse, or she would give them away to people who wandered into the shop after closing to deliver things or messages.

"What have you been doing out so late for work? What was the trip to the harbour district about?" she asked. "Chasing someone, you said?"

Perrin told her what had happened. He got the feeling that as he spoke, by the way she nodded, that aspects of the story were familiar to her.

"I have heard of those cat people," she said when he finished. "They haven't come into my shop, but some people who run businesses closer to the harbour have mentioned things about them. They always wear a face covering that only shows their eyes, so people can't see what they look like. They're definitely from the realms and they have a reputation for being involved with shady deals. If the Bureau is going to stop them, that's very good."

"We'll need better proof of wrongdoing for that. People from the realms can legally come to Tamba. There is no need for anyone to hide their identity, although there is no law that says that they can't wear face coverings."

"But they're magical, shady people."

"As inspectors, we also can't assume that someone who is from the realms is here for a shady deal just because they come from over there. We need solid proof."

"Well, those are the stories I hear from my friends and people who own shops, and in my book, there is usually at least some truth in rumours."

"Yes, there is, and it doesn't mean the Bureau won't listen to those stories. What else do the rumours say?"

She gave him an uneasy glance. While Dorella and her tea shop had a business as harmless and cute as a business could be, she would, for some supplies, have to rely on other, less wholesome operators. She had previously been a good source of information for him.

She sipped from her tea.

"Mind you, I have never faced any of these cat people in my life and I have no desire to have anything to do with them. But you don't always have the choice. If a business is desperate to have money paid to them, especially if it's a larger business, they might hire these people. They're known to work as debt collectors."

"But Tamba has our own debt collectors. Most businesses would go to the Office of Finance and hang their claims on the board outside for all to see. That usually fixes unpaid bills."

"And what about debts for services that they can't claim by posting a notice?"

"Well, then we're talking about something else entirely. We're talking about people who do illegal stuff. Not honest people."

"That is what I'm talking about. People hire magical debt collectors, because they have no other way of getting their debts paid."

"Well..." Perrin spread his hands. Types of debt collection and magic used in them were not his specialty. That's what the accountants downstairs in the building were for.

He didn't think there were businesses that would use this type of service without also being involved in other shady practices, but yes, in theory a business could be owed money from outside Tamba and there would be little point in posting a notice on the board outside the department of finance.

In theory.

Yes, there probably were those businesses. And they were most likely to be in the harbour district.

"Do you know anyone who would hire these services?"

"What? Me?"

She gave him a horrified look that answered the question.

"Just rumours, right?"

"Yes." Her cheeks had gone red. "There are people who use these services. If you're doing business, you will hear about them sooner or later."

Perrin didn't think that was the entire story, but he let it rest.

This issue needed time. Time for something to get out of hand and parties to be referred to the authorities.

He wasn't looking forward to it.

He went upstairs to his room a bit later when he finished his tea and Dorella needed to complete her accounting.

CHAPTER 5

When Perrin came into the office the next morning, the table that usually held pieces of paper with each inspector's work schedule for that day displayed a sign about a pre-work meeting.

So they all waited in the big office. While they waited, inspectors who had already gone home yesterday evening heard about the event in the harbour from colleagues.

Inspector Carbin read out the official report she had filed with the council about the happenings of the previous evening. It was a rather sanitised version of events, so she elaborated by giving more details.

She had also received a report from the guards, which included the names of people who had been questioned by the cat people. Strangely enough, there were few familiar names on that list.

A railway labourer. The owner of a small shop that sold bric-a-brac and secondhand goods. Dock workers.

There was no obvious connection between them.

Did that woman ever sleep?

She also announced that she had asked someone from the Investigator office to talk about what they were dealing with.

Perrin stood at the door of the rather cramped meeting room where Tyro told the group of gathered inspectors that the cat people called themselves pumans and they came from the realm of Rimindi. That magical realm traded little with Tamba. It was a landlocked region on the other side of the mountains. It was not a land of great riches, and Perrin understood they relied on Solania for a lot of their supplies.

But Tyro also said, "Pumans can be extremely dangerous and we should avoid dealing with them unless we have no other option. They answer only to their group's leader. They live in family groups of a handful of individuals, called a pride, and do not otherwise accept authority. They may have a reputation as debt collectors, but more often work for themselves under the guise of being debt collectors for others, meaning that they will collect the debt but then fail to pass it on to the people who are paying for its collection. In our limited experience, they're nothing but trouble. It's going to be vitally important that we find out what they want if we want them to leave."

"Certainly, we're not going to give in to a bunch of criminals," Inspector Carbin said. "It would help greatly if we can find out what they want, so that we can seize it and send it back to whatever realm it came from."

Perrin relayed what Dorella had told him, with Tyro nodding all the way through.

"Yes, puman debt collectors are a bit of a myth. Businesses in town will even threaten each other with the potential of hiring them if a dispute drags out. In truth, few people would know how to hire them, and even fewer would command their respect. People on the street talk about the "cat people" but few, if any, would have dealt with them directly. Pumans just don't come out and advertise that they can be hired to ruffle the customers who are late paying their bills. These people are very secretive. They will give their names and identities at the border or at the port wherever they come in, but most of the time those identities are not trackable, and they don't have a clear place of residence that we can make a complaint to. Sometimes they leave trails of dead bodies, especially those who are the subject of their claims. It's not the first time that they have come to Tamba. Every now and then, one of the merchants or someone in authority runs afoul of someone in the realms, and if that particular person is rich enough or angry enough, they may employ pumans. They don't come cheap."

"So it is all about finding out who owes what and making sure that they pay up?" Inspector Carbin said.

"Well, it's usually not that easy. Very often there are disputes about business contracts, often on the very margins of what's allowed, and since the Bureau doesn't get involved in commercial businesses, we usually can't take action, but yes we can pressure the parties into finding some sort of a solution that makes these bandits go away. The main issue for the Bureau is that the pumans may be after the subject of a claim, but while they're here, they often find extra ways to create trouble. They don't usually have or use money, so they end up stealing things, or they end up threatening people surrounding those that are the subject of the claim and very often, these are innocent people. The pumans are not easy to deal with. They stick to themselves and they don't like talking to anyone."

Inspector Carbin said, "Following on from what Tyro said, it's important that we find out what they're doing here. Finding out starts with proper reporting, so I want all of you who came with me yesterday to file your own individual reports. Write up what you remember from last night. Don't compare notes with others, but deliver the reports straight to me. I want everyone else to be super vigilant from now on."

According to the reports delivered by the guards, the pumans hadn't communicated with anyone what they were looking for and why they roughed up random people and why a railway labourer, a small shop owner and two dock workers qualified as subjects for their dubious questioning methods.

Inspector Carbin said that she would keep in close contact with the guards in case more information came out.

None of the other inspectors had noticed the pumans as visitors in any of the inns and guest houses they had inspected during the normal course of their work.

"Is there any way we can engage them in conversation?" Perrin said. "If we happen to come across them in our regular work, we could start a friendly chat. It's in their interest if we can get all parties to cooperate so that the debt gets paid or the dispute is solved, right?"

Tyro said, "You can try to engage them in conversation if you see them, but I wouldn't rate your chances too high. These guys don't chat over cups of tea. They avoid talking to anyone, and if they do, they are likely to lie. On top of that, you can never be sure that pumans are in Tamba to collect debt. It's unlikely to be their main business."

"Then what else do they do?" Perrin asked.

Tyro met Perrin's eyes. "They're so secretive, we're unsure what their most important source of income is. It's likely to be something illegal, something magical, or something relating to the proceeds of crime."

So after the meeting broke up, Perrin wrote up his report from what he had seen and went into Inspector Carbin's office to deliver it to her.

But while he went on his regular round of inspections of inns, he couldn't shake a feeling of disquiet. If Dorella, a sweet middle-aged lady with not a devious bone in her body, knew about these characters, the problem was likely to be worse than it at first appeared.

He'd do some of his own investigations.

Verbena lived in the harbour district, and he asked her to keep an eye out when she walked past the inn on her way to and from work to see if she could spot the pumans again, and follow them to where they were staying.

CHAPTER 6

Not much happened over the next few days, so Perrin returned to his normal work of going around the inns and inspecting the kitchens.

He encountered nothing unusual, and no matter how much he looked, he didn't see any suspicious characters.

He also spent some time looking after all his magic sniffers, because the young ones were about to make their appearance, and he needed to keep the cages clean and the animals well fed.

Every evening, when he returned home, he heard the normal type of things from Dorella while they shared a cup of tea, and they talked about all kinds of things. He asked a few times about the puman cat people, but Dorella could not give him any more news than what she had already told him.

And now that he thought about it, Dorella's knowledge was likely to be dated. She might have once mingled with people who knew about pumans, but he hadn't asked her how long ago she had heard the information.

Verbena walked past the harbourside inn every morning and evening but didn't see anything worth reporting either.

Perrin almost dared hope that the puman people had left town and he would not have to worry about them anymore.

But of course, that was only wishful thinking.

On an evening about three days later, he was walking home and picking up a few things from the shops on the way home, when he saw a suspiciously familiar character about a block ahead of him. It was not so much that he knew the individual, but that he recognised the fluid and soundless way he walked. Like a cat.

He sped up until he walked right behind the man and yes, when he turned his head sideways ever so slightly, Perrin could see the edges of the black mask painted with silver.

A couple of shoppers coming the other way raised their eyebrows, but strange characters from the realms were no uncommon sight in the central shopping district of Tamba, and many of those wore face coverings to hide their unusual features.

Perrin kept back a little and followed along to see what this person was doing. He was alone and didn't seem to care about being followed. A cloth bag containing a small item swung from his arm. Perrin didn't see weapons on his belt.

About halfway up the street, he turned to a nondescript shopfront along the street and went in through its dusty door. Perrin was going to wait across the road in an alley, when a second puman came out of that alley, crossed the main street and went into the shop as well.

Well, that was a bit of luck that Perrin hadn't followed too closely. They would have noticed him.

He waited in the porch of a groceries shop further back.

Perrin was not familiar with the business where the pumans had gone. The building looked old and in need of maintenance. There was no sign either in the shop window or on the door that indicated the type of business conducted inside.

The main street held a few of those places, businesses from

bygone eras, where someone still paid the rent, where the owners stored spare items, or where the shopfront was a cover for another business like a bookkeeping business, and where competing shop owners hadn't yet offered the right price for the building to change hands.

This one looked like one of those old-fashioned bric-a-brac secondhand places that sold whatever weird and wonderful items they could lay their hands on.

But if so, the shop put very little effort into selling their wares. The window display was boxed off with a plank of wood blocking the view into what would be the shop window. The area above the plank was dark, showing only the glow of a single light within.

The window was dirty with grime. The paint on the door and window frame was peeling.

He waited and waited.

He was standing for so long in front of the grocery shop that the owner came out to ask him if he wanted to buy anything.

Perrin said he didn't, and then when the shop owner kept looking at him, felt compelled to move along. Not that there was an obvious place to hide.

He pulled his hat over the side of his face because he had to go past the dingy shop, and hoped that the puman people inside the shop wouldn't see his inspectors uniform.

He peeked into the shop while walking through the street.

It was very dark inside. A yellowed piece of paper stuck to the inside of the window. It said, *Outside shop hours, please knock. The bell doesn't work.*

That boded well.

What would people want here outside shop hours, anyway? An emergency purchase of second hand rubbish? It didn't look like anyone visited the place, even during shop hours.

He waited in front of another shop where the windows were

dark and everyone had gone home for the day, until eventually the two pumans came out into the dusk, and disappeared at a trot across the street and into the alley.

Now what should he do? Follow them or go into the shop?

He was alone and not on duty. He wasn't much good at climbing or running, or, heaven forbid, fighting. If he followed and something happened, then Inspector Carbin would have his hide. He'd become acquainted with that unpleasant experience in the past, and it was not one he was keen to repeat.

So, go into the shop then.

Because he also felt that if he relayed this story tomorrow, someone would have expected him to do *something*.

Perrin crossed the street and climbed the low step to the door.

He half expected—or hoped?—it to be locked, but it opened with nothing more than a creak. Right. The bell didn't work.

Behind the grime-covered door in desperate need of a coat of paint, he found a cluttered shop with bare floorboards, shelves and tables full of randomly stacked items, ranging from old books to blackened silver cutlery, to dusty mismatched glasses, to little tables and chairs. Some were still in boxes, some of them stacked on top of each other and shoved under the display tables.

The owner of the shop sat behind the counter at the back wall. He was an old man with wispy grey hair. His face was utterly unfamiliar to Perrin. He shrunk into the corner, wide-eyed, when Perrin came in.

"I didn't buy anything from them, I swear," he said. His voice cracked with age.

"I haven't even asked my question yet," Perrin said.

"No, but you're here because of those weird people who came in here just now, right? I have nothing to do with them, I swear!"

"Calm down, calm down. I did see them coming in, but I'm

not interested in your business, but I'd like to know what they're after and what they asked you."

"I don't know, I swear. I have nothing to do with them." His eyes were wide. "I'm an honest man. I don't have anything to do with that... magic stuff. You can search my shop if you want."

Perrin looked around. Now that his eyes had become used to the dimness, even more of the mess in the shop was clear. Boxes stood on the floor, a variety of secondhand rubbish spilling out. Search that? Er. No.

"I'm also much less interested in your business than in their business."

The man stared at him, as if he was a mouse disturbed at night in the kitchen while eating the cheese.

Perrin continued, "Why were they here? Do you have a debt to anyone?"

"Me? No. I always pay everything on time. They said they were looking for stolen items that might have been sold on to secondhand shops... I asked them what item they were looking for so I could help them, but they wanted to see everything I had. Look at the mess they made." His voice shook.

He gestured at a couple of open boxes on the floor, all of them with a jumble of items inside. Several items also lay on the floor, ranging from old forks to a rusty compass, two unused notebooks with yellowing paper and many other pieces of junk.

"I'm only an old man. I don't have big, expensive things. Nothing like they would come out of the realms to find."

Perrin walked over and took a peek at the stuff on the floor. He couldn't imagine that anyone would pay much for this junk that looked to have been sitting in these boxes for many years.

He picked up an old book. The covers were so faded that it was difficult to read the title, especially in the darkness. He opened it. The yellowed pages appeared to contain children's bedtime stories. He was about to put it back in the box when something caught his attention.

A white porcelain teapot with tiny pink flowers painted on the round belly. If he was not mistaken, this came from the same vendor where Atreyo and his family bought their tableware, and he knew this because Mirella had perused the catalogues extensively when she got married.

He picked it up. It was dusty, but complete. It had probably been dumped here because at some point it had become separated from its matching cups.

But Dorella adored this sort of stuff.

He carried it over to the counter.

"These strangers, did they threaten you?"

"Don't know what you call threatening. Did they grab me or point a knife at me? No. But they said that if it turned out that I was lying about having stuff and they found anything, they would take it and they would force me to pay a fine."

"So they did threaten you. How can you fail to let them know about something if they don't tell you what they're looking for?"

"See? You understand! That's the problem. They came to harass me, an old man who has done nothing wrong, and make unreasonable demands that I have no hope of meeting. It's all about lording it over us shopkeepers."

"Whatever they're doing, they're not allowed to be in Tamba."

"It didn't look like they cared a lot about that. I'm just an old man selling a few things, you know? I have no interest in trying to play games with people from the realms. Did that in my youth. Got the scars, too."

"Well..." Perrin shrugged and looked around the messy shop. "Put everything back on the shelves. They obviously found nothing. But for the future, remember this. I am Perrin and I'm a magic inspector from the Bureau of Magic Abuse. If ever something similar happens or you hear anything that disturbs you, report it to the Bureau. There is not much point in leaving these characters to sow terror on the streets and letting them get away with it by keeping quiet about it. That's not how we lead our lives in Tamba." Then he gestured at the counter. "How much for the teapot?"

CHAPTER 7

When Perrin came home with the teapot, Dorella was in the kitchen doing the washing up.

"Late again?" she said, with her back to the door.

"Yes. I have something for you."

"Oh?" Now she turned around, wiping her hands on her apron.

Perrin took the teapot from his bag. "I thought you might like this." He held it out. Just now, he noticed it was a bit dusty.

"Oh, you silly. It's gorgeous, but you shouldn't have to do this. The shop does well enough for me to buy my own teapots."

"Sorry, it's a bit dusty. I should have cleaned it first."

"Oh, I have just the thing to fix that. I bought this at the markets a while back."

She opened a cupboard and took out a bottle with a syrupy concoction inside.

"It seemed like a good buy to clean things, and he was demonstrating it at the stand. It worked beautifully."

"Dorella?"

"What?" She turned around, her face red.

She spread her hands and let them sink again. Her eyes glittered.

"I really don't need a teapot. I'm a bit..." She shrugged. "I'm sorry."

"Don't be. It was a little thing. I saw it for sale while at work and thought you might like it."

"It's not a little thing at all. Nobody ever buys me presents."

"Well, this can be our teapot when we have tea together. If I ever find any cups and plates that match it, I'll buy them, too."

"That would be lovely. Just a teapot for after work. Not a work teapot."

That settled the matter, and when Perrin came back from work the next day, he found the teapot all scrubbed and shiny, sitting on the table in the corner where they usually sat, with a set of pink tea cups and matching plates, which rather suited the ensemble.

She wanted to know where he had bought the teapot so she could chase up the rest of the set.

"The cups might have been broken," Perrin said.

"I doubt it. I know these types of people. They're very precious with their tableware. Probably someone thought they could make more money selling them separately."

Probably.

So Perrin told her about the old fellow and his dingy old shop.

Dorella, being Dorella, then offered some gossip about him, which confirmed what Perrin had already observed: that he'd owned the place for a long time, that he had inherited the business from his father who used to run a thriving clothes shop, but the son had little interest in dealing with staff and all the suppliers and the council, or going to fairs to sell fancy clothing. He was unmarried and lived at the back of the shop.

Perrin thought that would be the last he saw of the old fellow.

He went back to his inspections, and over the next few days, on his way home, glanced at the shop but never saw anything else that disturbed him, nor any sign that the owner had been sufficiently shaken by the experience to clean his windows and at least make an effort to appeal to the general public.

He fully expected never to see the old man again, and for a few days, he didn't, and his life became consumed by another, bigger problem. Shall we say, a dragon-sized problem.

Because in a previous adventure, he'd seized an illegal stash of dragon eggs and a baby dragon. The Bureau had packed up the eggs and shipped them back to Solania a long time ago. But you couldn't just put a dragon in a box and let the mail service deliver it, even if you had a delivery address, and that was another story all by itself.

Dragons came from Solania, but even within that realm, no one owned dragons. No one even liked dragons. They could be useful. They were often a menace, but there were many dragons in the Solanian mountains, and no one in Solania could be suffi-ciently bothered by the presence of one of *their* dragons in another realm to cooperate with—or pay for—measures to send it back.

And, to add to the problem, what had once been a baby dragon quickly became a larger dragon. Dragons were strong and had vicious claws that could rip through timber walls, that could prise open doors, that could bend rods of metal, as the dragon in question had demonstrated repeatedly.

Dragons also had a foul temper and farts that made even the most determined dragon tamer run for the exit. And dragon tamers were in short supply in Tamba in the first place.

Perrin had tried putting the beast on a truck, but a burnt-out truck and an angry transport operator later, the dragon was back in town. He even counted himself lucky that they'd been able to trick the beast into entering a storage crate and they'd been able to catch it.

He'd finally put the beast on the train back to Solania, in the company of a specially-trained handler and enclosed in a fortified cage.

Stupidly maybe, he had assumed it would be the last he saw of the beast...

Or that his life would remain as calmly in control as it was that one particular afternoon when he returned from his inspections.

As he plonked the cage with the magic sniffers on his desk, he became aware of a disturbance in the office at the back of the room, Inspector Carbin's office, where a man raised his voice.

In that office, behind the windows, Inspector Carbin sat at her desk with her arms crossed over her chest and a man stood on the other side of her desk, waving his hands as he shouted at her. Perrin couldn't see his face and didn't recognise his voice, but he wore a railway uniform.

"What's going on?" Perrin asked his colleague on the next desk.

"I don't know. He was in the office when I came back. They were already shouting at each other then."

"They were talking about paying damages," another colleague said.

"For what?" someone else asked.

The first man shrugged. "I didn't hear that."

But a deep sense of suspicion crept over Perrin, because this wouldn't be the first time that infernal dragon created trouble.

Oh, no, not again.

He wanted this very much not to be about the dragon. He wanted to be rid of the dragon, as he should be, because a dragon, being a magical creature, was obviously not allowed to be in Tamba, and it should go back to where it came from. But in the past few months, a lot in his job had been about the dragon, at the most inopportune moments.

And he'd been so sure he'd finally banished that dragon out of his life, and here it was again.

At that moment, Inspector Carbin looked out the window into the main office. Her eyes met Perrin's. She rose from the desk and strode to the door.

"Perrin, can you come in here?"

Oh, yes, definitely. This was about the dragon.

Under the curious stares of all those in the large office room, he walked through the aisle between the desks to Inspector Carbin's office.

The visitor's expression barely remained polite as Perrin entered and shut the door behind him, enclosing the three in a tense silence.

"This is officer Parvo from the railway freight despatch office," Inspector Carbin began. "Officer, this is Inspector Perrin, our inspector in charge of this matter. Perrin, I'm afraid there has been a bit of an issue."

"I'm guessing it's about the dragon," Perrin said.

"*Your* dragon." Parvo's nostrils flared. His face was still red from arguing with Inspector Carbin.

"It's nobody's dragon, which is part of the problem," Perrin said. "It came from Solania, but it doesn't belong to—"

"Excuse me, this is *your* dragon. You told us to transport a crate. The contents of the crate are yours. We only look after the delivery of the goods to the nominated address. We do not tamper with the contents of the crates. This is *your* crate and *your* dragon. And *your* beast has now destroyed two crates and the interior of a train carriage."

"It destroyed the crate? But how could that have happened? We used the strongest crate we could find."

"You tell me. We put the crate on the train as agreed."

"Did you allow the handler in the carriage?"

"Yes. We did everything as we discussed. The animal handler would agree with me if he had the opportunity, but was so distraught, he's resigned on the spot and has left town, leaving us short an animal handler for the transport of less troublesome creatures that we actually make money transporting on trains, like horses. Now, what am I going to do?"

Inspector Carbin snorted. "Find another animal handler. That is not our problem. Get on with the story and tell the inspector what happened and what you want from us."

Parvo shot her an angry look.

"What happened is clear. This dreadful creature started to destroy your 'strongest ever' crate before we were even out of town. It had escaped before the train was out of the country. Fortunately, the driver noticed and could stop the train and could turn around in time so we could put it back in the cage. You can be lucky that the carriage was made from steel and the dragon hadn't yet worked out how to open the door or it would have escaped into the city."

"Did you follow all our instructions?"

"Yes! But instructions are no good when facing a dragon that's so angry it has flames coming out of its ears. At that time, instructions are nothing. When you're facing a menace that is worse than hell itself, and you're on a moving train with no help. That was the predicament my poor employee found himself in and that caused him to leave his job. Now I'm short on qualified workers. Because of *your* dragon." He glared at Inspector Carbin and then at Perrin.

"You have animal handlers. You assured us that you could take care of it," Inspector Cabin said.

"Well, I'm here to inform you that we are done with this

dragon. You come to pick it up and take it out of our warehouse. We're not dealing with it anymore."

"Where are we going to put it? Up here in the office?" Perrin protested.

"I don't care. We have suffered enough losses and terrorising of our mail room and transport staff. I've lost people because of this beast. Can I also remind you that it set fire to a mail delivery, it escaped and upset the mail storage area so that we had to spend three days sorting it. And now this. We're a mail office, not an animal facility." He looked pointedly at Perrin's cage with the magic sniffers that still stood on his desk.

Inspector Carbin snorted. "Well, if you would just take steps to keep the dragon in the cage—"

"Don't you think we haven't tried? You should have seen the long list of all the things we told the rail employees not to do. As you might realise, a dragon is not just another parcel you can pick up and put wherever you want."

"I do realise that," Inspector Carbin said, sounding prim. "You still advertise yourself as being a facility that deals with the transport of animals. As far as I know, the dragon is an animal."

"I don't think you realise anything at all. I don't think the Bureau has any idea what they're dealing with. Just send it on the train, those were your very words. There is nothing *just* about a dragon, not even a baby one that's rapidly becoming a big angry dragon."

"Instead of arguing about it, can you suggest something we can do about it?" Perrin said.

"It's got to leave my warehouse!" Parvo's face had gone red again. The spit flew out of his mouth. "We won't put up with this... this *creature* any longer!"

"We're just going to walk it down the street and put it up in an inn, right?"

Parvo glared at Perrin, and Perrin glared back.

"I think you do understand the problem," he then said. "You just want someone else, and not the Bureau, to be saddled with it."

"Inspector Carbin is right: you advertised yourself to us as an animal handling facility. Forgive us for *not* being an animal handling facility. That's why we hired you: to look after it. But if you want to break your contract, we will need some time to—"

"No. No more time. No more excuses. I want the beast gone. We're part of the mail office, not the Bureau of Magic Abuse. We look after goats and pigeons, sheep and horses. We don't know how to keep a dragon. We don't know what to feed a dragon. And, to be perfectly fair with you, our charter does not cover the shipment of dragons. My staff have no training in the handling of dragons."

"It still needs to be sent back to Solania, for the safety of all citizens of Tamba. We're all doing our civil duty, and we are not equipped for handling dragons, either. We all need to do our part. Especially if we're paid to do it."

"Maybe so, but it won't be staying in our storage facilities. You can have your money back. Take that beast out of my warehouse. Today. If not gone by tomorrow morning, our charge for holding it will double, and if it's not gone the day after, it will double again, and this will continue until it's gone. And if you don't make a serious attempt to pick the beast up, or you're stalling deliberately, I will release it, and then we'll see how quickly you can act."

CHAPTER 8

Officer Parvo would not persuaded to make a compromise, ridiculous as his demands were. The dragon had to be gone today. Of course, he was also right about his office being unprepared to care for a dragon, and both Perrin and Inspector Carbin understood that.

The poor man and his staff had dealt with most of the animal's misbehaviour for the past few months. But they had also happily taken the Bureau's money to look after it while the Bureau found a way of returning the beast to Solania.

So after Parvo had left the office in big angry strides, with the threat that he'd release the dragon if no one came to pick it up, Inspector Carbin told Perrin that he had better start making arrangements to find somewhere else for the dragon as soon as possible.

Inspector Carbin said, "I very much doubt he will actually release the animal, but he'll definitely double his charges. And we're on a tight enough budget already and I don't want to have to go to the council to explain why the beast is still here—"

Perrin opened his mouth—

"Yes, I know and understand the difficulties we've had, but we really need to move on a resolution to our dragon problem."

"But how are we going to get it back to Solania?" Perrin asked. "We tried the courier and didn't work. We tried the train and that didn't work. And each of those attempts was a major effort, with people building the crates and the downstairs office applying for thousands of permits. The only option I can see left to us is to hire a magician, but that won't go down well with the council or the citizens. Some people tell us to just release the beast, but no one can assure us that the dragon will go home. In fact, there is evidence to the contrary. This dragon hatched here. The first creature it saw was probably a local cat or something, or, heaven forbid, some miscreant in the harbour district. The dragon considers Tamba its home, and once we release it, there is no catching it if it decides to hang around."

"I know, I know." She raised her hands. "But we need to solve it. Grandmaster Yorick is still expecting the beast to return to Solania, yes?"

"As far as I know. I mean, he's not been very communicative..."

Grandmaster Yorick was a whole different chapter all by himself.

"Look, Perrin, give this top priority. I can take you off inspections until the beast is safely gone. It shouldn't take you very long once you can dedicate all your time to the problem, if I give you all the time you need."

"And the resources?" Meaning: money.

"And resources."

Perrin heaved a sigh.

"I don't know, but I'll do my best, I guess."

"No, not guess. This time, we have to really get rid of it. You have become one of my most trusted employees. I rely on you to solve this problem."

Perrin returned to his desk, his mind filled with despair about the insurmountable problem he faced.

Where would he find someone with the equipment and knowledge to safely transport the dragon, given that he didn't trust magicians?

Dealing with the ancient Solanian magician Yorick had been a challenge by itself. The man was hard to pin down, evasive and condescending in his correspondence.

Perrin pulled out the two letters he had received from the man, written in such an elaborate style that the text was barely legible.

Apparently, the grandmaster said, it was Tamba's fault that the dragon was in town because "there are no magical protections" and "clearly you need a half-decent magician to save you from yourselves."

Perrin had discarded many rudely-written responses to those words.

The grandmaster had, however, and no doubt grudgingly, agreed in black and white to rehabilitate the dragon once Perrin could get it to Solania, because the grandmaster had explicitly stated that travel to Tamba—that most dull and drab of places, he said—was beneath him or the officials of the Solanian grand council and as such he thought that "The time and efforts of members of the Solanian council are better spent on matters that concern the Solanian people."

And those people, it transpired, didn't care much for dragons. They had plenty of other dragons and felt no particular ownership towards this one.

Apparently also Solania had a law against the export of dragon eggs to prevent a situation just like the one they found themselves in.

Perrin had tried so very hard to ask for one of the grandmaster's disciples to come and help transport the beast with more forceful means than the pitiful thunderstaff that Perrin had, which was little more than a cattle prod in disguise and only resulted in making the dragon angry these days.

But Grandmaster Yorick was a master in obfuscation, and for every letter Perrin wrote, he would take ages simply to send an infuriatingly vague response, or worse, have his bureaucrats send a vague response.

This had gone on far too long.

So instead of going home—he'd looked forward to getting one of Dorella's cakes—he went to the harbour front railway freight storage warehouse.

The department that dealt with animals was at the back of the building, a large open hall where the smell of straw wafted out of the doorway.

A few horses stood in their pens, and two men were moving barriers so that the animals could be led into the train carriage that waited on the other side.

There were also a couple of crates that contained fat white geese, sticking their necks through the openings and making their displeasure about being caged up known.

A peacock in a cage next to the geese sat in the straw, its head tucked under its wing, ignoring the noise made by its neighbours. The magnificent tail—all folded up—was scrunched against the side of the bars.

Further into the warehouse, a female employee was trying to coax two donkeys out of their pens to walk through the hall and into a train carriage.

Both animals were extremely restless, snorting and tossing their heads.

"Ah, you're the guy from the Bureau," she said, meeting Perrin's eyes. "I'll be glad when that monster is gone. Loading the horses takes twice as long. They're that nervous. Go on, take the wretched thing out of here."

She jerked her head in the direction of the back wall.

In this place stood a large crate made from thick wooden beams fortified with bars of iron that surrounded the structure.

A grate made of similarly thick iron bars sat at eye level, and from within the darkness beyond came the sound of snorting and scuffling.

As Perrin came closer, followed by the young employee from the front office, an eye appeared behind that tiny window. The iris was vivid orange, the pupil slitted like a cat's.

There was also—and Perrin hadn't seen this before—a smattering of bright gold spots in the iris. It could be a trick of the light in this shed, or... He'd read that a dragon's eye colour indicated its health. He had to look it up once he finally got home.

The dragon's head angled in a way that suggested that it curved its neck in order to look through the opening, that the rest of its body was much taller, pushing the ceiling of the crate.

That beast grew bigger by the day.

It blew out a breath, and while its nostrils were behind the wall of the crate and not visible through the tiny window, Perrin could hear the loud huff and smell the hot air.

Perrin had read in his books that dragons only breathed fire if they ate a lot of meat, so he'd instructed the handlers to give the creature pumpkins, because they were in season, but this led to a new problem: a vegetarian dragon was not a happy dragon.

A diet of pumpkins was also not a long term healthy situation.

The eye moved as the young man led Perrin past the crate. It was disturbing, as if the beast knew him.

That dragon was getting horribly big pretty fast.

"Don't go too close," the man said.

Perrin had no such intention. The smell of the hot breath was enough to put him off.

The young man continued, "The beast is much smarter than

you'd think. It hates us. The other day, one of my workers walked past, and it turned around in the cage, pressing its rear end to the window. And then... not to be too crude, but if you'd want to clear a building, dragon farts are a very good way of doing it. The smell!"

"The gas would make them a fire hazard," Perrin said.

The man gave him a suspicious look, as if he was working out whether Perrin was serious or having him on. A bit of both, probably.

In a way, he felt sorry for the creature. It should be in the Solanian mountains, soaring over the peaks, catching mountain goats or whatever dragons ate. At any rate, not eating pumpkins —no offense to the pumpkins.

The employee led him to the side of the shed.

"See, here we have a crane strong enough to lift the crate with the dragon inside. You can back a cart or a truck in here."

Perrin looked at the mechanism of metal beams, hooks, chains and pulleys. It looked sturdy, and he knew the railway moved shipments of marble and iron.

Getting the dragon out of here was not that hard. Keeping it under control once it was on the train was the issue.

But why?

Did it not understand what was happening and did it panic?

"I first need to find an alternative place to house it," he said.

"That should be easy. There are plenty of warehouses around."

"It will need to be close to the station, so we get the crate on the train—"

"No."

"What, no?"

"We're the providers of animal transport carriages and we're not taking the beast anymore." He stood with his hands planted at his sides. "I thought our boss had made that clear."

"But I still need to get it out of here."

"You'll have to find some other way."

Perrin had already tried a truck, but that hadn't worked so well, either. "Surely, there are other railway transport providers?"

"None that I know of that deal with animals. You could get some dodgy operator if you're lucky. I don't know. I don't care."

"Then what do you suggest I do?" Perrin spread his hands.

"Get a truck."

"We've tried a truck already! It didn't even make it out of the city. The owner complained about the weight, and that has only increased."

"You could use a boat. The weight wouldn't be an issue."

Huh.

A boat.

That was an option Perrin hadn't yet considered. Solania was on the coast. Travel was shorter overland, but the boat was a possibility.

But it would need to be a big boat.

And the dragon would have to remain on the deck for quite a few days. He'd also have to find someone willing to take the dragon on, and that was going to be hard after the two mishaps.

It would also be expensive to hire a boat of the right size. And it would take time to find one. Possibly more time than he had. He knew very little about boats.

But he had travelled on boats with Atreyo. And as far as he remembered, Atreyo's brother had interests that involved boats.

It was definitely something worth considering.

After assuring the man he'd remove the dragon as soon as he could, Perrin went to scope out some warehouses for temporarily housing a dragon, and he was mostly informed that they didn't cater for live animals—he didn't even mention that the animal would be a dragon, although one or two of the owners were suspicious about someone from the Bureau of Magic Abuse asking for animal housing, while in uniform. Did the Bureau not look after their own magic sniffers, a man asked. Perrin wasn't sure if he was serious. But he was carrying the cage with the magic sniffers after all.

He found an owner who didn't seem to care much about what he stored, but this man didn't seem to care much about anything else either, including the state of the building and the fact that the only access road to it wound between two other warehouses and the alley was so full of rubbish that it would need to cleared before a truck with the crate could pass.

Also, Perrin would need to find his own people to look after the dragon while he frantically sought a way to get the beast back to Solania.

There was a distinct shortage of dragon handlers in town. Or just any kind of animal handlers who didn't run at the sound of the word *dragon*.

It grew late and later still. He grew hungry and cranky. His arm grew tired from carrying the magic sniffers, and the poor things were getting annoyed as well. They needed to be fed.

So he gave up and went home. Whether Parvo was bluffing about releasing the dragon or not, Perrin couldn't do anything about it. The Bureau had one cage suitable for a dragon, the dragon was in it, and moving it elsewhere was not easy.

CHAPTER 9

Perrin's next couple of days were filled with trying to find another spot for the dragon, and finding handlers, and when he finally found these things, in a warehouse in the not so very illustrious harbour district, then finding transport to move the dragon there.

This required a large wagon with a flat bed. The mail office warehouse had a crane, but the place where it was to be moved did not, so he needed to find one of those as well, unless he wanted to pay for hiring the truck and park it and the dragon in the warehouse for as long as it took him to find another solution.

It infuriated him that both the truck and the crane belonged to the railways, whose services Parvo said he couldn't use, except when calling it "private contracts". This included paying more than twice the regular rate, having to do it after hours—supposedly for "safety", but more likely because those "private" contracts could only use the crane and wagon after the railway employees had gone home and no longer needed them, and probably also with tacit knowledge of their bosses.

Perrin spent a lot of time dealing with this, and it was time he didn't get to spend with his magic sniffers, including Frida's impending litter. She was getting bigger and bigger. The brood would need a new cage, and he should also think about selling some of his other animals to businesses that imported a lot of their wares. But although people had expressed an interest in buying magic sniffers, he didn't want to sell them to just anyone, and he also didn't want to break any laws while doing it.

Magic sniffers were not magical creatures. They were large mountain rats that lived in proximity to dragons and had developed sensors to detect dragons, because dragons ate magic sniffers and detecting dragons as early as possible was a matter of survival.

But magic sniffers came from Solania, and anything that came out of that realm was viewed with suspicion in Tamba. On top of that, things that came from Solania might become the subject of random claims from Solania's mercurial Grandmaster Yorick as soon as he got a whiff that something from his realm was worth money outside Solania. Dragons were not worth money. They cost money.

Perrin wanted to pre-empt claims from Solania before advertising his magic sniffers for sale. Which also meant he needed to build a new cage for Frida's almost-adult brood.

But that infernal dragon occupied all his time. It was growing rapidly and would soon be too big for the only cage the Bureau owned that was big enough to contain it.

Contrary to what he'd been told by Parvo and the official railway operator, Perrin found a different, private, railcar business who would consider transporting a dragon. They specialised in carrying horses and cattle and other agricultural animals. This company's office was at the edge of town, where one might find these types of animals.

Perrin went to visit it, but while the owner said he was keen,

Perrin wasn't impressed with the facilities. Oh, they were good enough for cows and horses, but Perrin didn't think the business owner appreciated how big and dangerous a dragon was.

The dragon in question, cooped up in the cage now installed in the new warehouse, grew increasingly impatient.

Perrin had gotten a chance to read up on the eye colours. Apparently, a dragon's eyes changed colour when it approached maturity. The gold flecking indicated that the animal was female. Wasn't that great? Because female dragons were the strongest and most aggressive, being the ones defending the nest.

And this poor dragon was treating the crate as its nest.

It made it impossible for the poor boy tasked with feeding the dragon and cleaning the cage, to shovel out the rather big and steamy dragon-doos. This was already a delicate task, achieved with the aid of two rakes with very long handles, that needed to be manoeuvred between the dragon's claws to pull the offending smelly object close enough to the metal grid to be able to push it out.

The dragon had developed the tendency to stomp on the rake handles so that they cracked and broke. Perrin was close to spending his annual materials budget just on replacing broom handles and was having a hard time convincing Inspector Carbin that he needed yet another broom handle.

Worryingly, the dragon then set fire to the handles, and to the poor handler's jacket, and the hay bales that were stacked against the side wall of the warehouse.

Perrin didn't believe it when he heard it. This was why they were feeding the dragon pumpkins, right? So that it wouldn't be able to spew fire.

He went to check at the warehouse, and yes, the boy had only fed the creature pumpkins.

"But it's getting really hard to clean the cage, mister."

"Use the rakes. Make them longer by tying the handles together."

"I already do. Wait. I'll show you."

He ran to the corner of the shed and came back with two metal rakes on some very long handles. Pulling with both hands, he opened the back cover of the crate where a heavy steel grate covered the opening. A waft of warm and smelly air came out.

Perrin covered his nose with his hand. "Phew, that stinks."

"You tell me about it, mister."

The kid was really brave beyond his years.

"What's your name?"

"Benno, sir."

"Be careful, Benno. This dragon is very angry."

The boy nodded. "Got to feed it first."

He grabbed a pumpkin off the wheelbarrow, snuck to the tiny side window, and worked the thing between the bars.

It toppled in and made a thump on the floor of the crate. The dragon snorted and glanced to the side.

Benno waited until the dragon turned around in the crate. That in itself was hard enough. Then he grabbed the broomsticks and snuck to the side of the crate. He stuck both rakes in between the bars and in quick succession manoeuvred two large poops out of the cage.

He was fishing for a third when the dragon stepped backwards and butted its rear end into the metal bars. Dragon butts were soft and fleshy, all muscle. And because it had folded its tail over its back, all of it was on display in full glory.

"See? This is what I mean!" Benno called out.

The handle of one of the rakes was stuck between the dragon's rear and the bars, and the dragon pushed against the metal with all its weight, rubbing the bars.

That lock wasn't going to hold.

"Shut the door!" he yelled out.

Benno grabbed the handle, but the door was heavy and wouldn't move quickly, and the dragon was still rubbing its back end into the bars, and then...

A jet of yellow fluid shot out, narrowly missing Benno. It flew across the space into the hay bales, and... hundreds of rats scurried out.

"Oh! Did you see how it just peed?" Benno yelled out.

See it, yes, but now Perrin could also smell it, too. Urgh.

Benno pushed the door shut while the last rats scrambled out of the hay bales.

Rats.

The dragon had been eating rats. That was why it could blow fire.

How could he get rid of rats? They were everywhere in the harbour.

Perrin's mind filled with despair. Earlier this year, he'd been so smug because he thought he'd solved this problem. Instead, he was back frantically racing time.

While the dragon was a nuisance now, this was nothing compared to what it would be like when it grew into full maturity. Particularly a female dragon, which needed to build a lair and attract mates.

After he had come home, he pulled out everything he could find about dragons in Atreyo's books. Apparently, the female dragon piss-squirted backwards when marking her den and getting ready to lay eggs. These behaviours were all very worrying signs of increasing maturity.

So he almost forgot all else and worked on, once again, getting rid of the dragon.

But the next day, when he came back to the office from visiting authorities to make things happen—did people realise what a stubborn and obstinate man the Solanian ambassador was?—he found that Inspector Carbin wanted to speak to him.

"There is a fellow for you downstairs," she said.

"I'm incredibly busy," Perrin said.

"I know, but he's asked to see you in particular. He says that he's had prior dealings with you. He didn't know your name, but we took a bit of time to try to find out who he was talking about, but eventually we figured out it must be you, because the description fitted."

Of course, there were not that many inspectors of Perrin's age, with most of the inspectors being very young.

The man had left his name, but it didn't mean anything to him. Had he dealt with this man?

Perrin went down to see the who this mysterious person was. He was surprised to find the old fellow from the dingy second hand shop that he'd seen the pumans visit.

Well, he'd almost forgotten about this affair.

The man had made an effort to dress up, but the coat he wore was old-fashioned and his white shirt had seen better days.

Before Perrin could welcome him, he said, "You told me to come and see you when anything happened."

Perrin checked himself. He didn't look that scary, did he?

"That's right. And I suppose something has happened?"

"Yes. But no, those strange people didn't come back, but somebody came to my shop to try and and sell something to me that was really strange. "

"Strange?"

"It's a collection, very old. There are some unusual items, not the usual kind of stuff I sell, if you get what I mean."

No, Perrin didn't get what he meant, but he took the old fellow into one of the private meeting rooms along the hall, and got him to describe the items and the person who was trying to sell them.

This turned out to be a woman, and one of high class at that. That in itself was suspicious.

Perrin wondered why somebody of high class needed to sell things to a shop quite as dingy as that, and the man said he didn't understand it either, which was why he had come to see the inspectors.

He said, "She seemed kind of nervous, you know, like she didn't want to be there, like all of this was beneath her."

Perrin nodded. He was well aware of the type of attitude. Even he, when he lived with Atreyo, had sometimes been subject to it. When people didn't realise whose partner he was, they would ask him to get drinks, as if he was a servant. The nobility was really very precious in protecting their special status, because when it really came to it, there wasn't that much to it. They were just normal people who did all the things that normal people did. They helped each other, they had fights, they did things that upset each other. They got hungry, they ate, they peed, got sick and at the end they died just like everyone else.

The fellow continued, "Anyway, this lady had this big box of things with her, and she opened it so that I could have a look to see if there was anything I wanted to buy. It was the most strange assortment of goods I've seen. I'm sure that most of it was highly illegal, items from the realms that she shouldn't have had."

Meaning: magical items.

"Did she say anything about how she acquired the items and why she wanted to sell them?"

"She said her husband had bought them in some sort of ill-fated business venture, but the items had given him no end of trouble, so she said she wanted to sell them without his knowledge before he could do any serious damage to himself or to his family."

"That would be the perfect reason for you not to buy them.

Don't get involved in relationships between these people, especially not between a married couple."

"That was my thought, and I couldn't see a clear market for these items either. So I didn't buy them."

"What sort of things were they?"

"Well, one of the things she seemed to think it was worth a lot of money was this rusty old trumpet that was completely encrusted with growths like it had been in the water at the bottom of the harbour for a while. She said that it was some kind of special item and that collectors would give a lot of money for it. I couldn't see how."

"Did you ask her why she then didn't sell it herself? Because if she said it was worth a lot of money, she would have known who told her this."

"I presume it was because she was afraid of her husband finding out and the two probably share a lot of the same social circles."

"So she was relying on you to secretly sell these items to someone she didn't know and to put a distance between her family and the items, which were probably illegal?"

"Something like that. I don't know. I didn't want to get involved. I told her I sell secondhand tableware and know nothing about items from the realms, and told her to go to some of the serious secondhand sellers. She seemed a bit disappointed, because I think she probably already tried that and they turned her down, too."

"Did she tell you her name, or did you know her?"

"No, I don't deal with those people, especially the women. I kind of respected that she didn't introduce herself, especially if she acted behind her husband's back. Who knows what other trouble she might be going through."

Perrin could fully appreciate that.

Still, for a high-class lady to go into a shop like his to try to sell something illegal was rather fishy. It might well be that this was the type of stuff that the puman people had been looking for, but without further information, and with all the other stuff going on, there was nothing Perrin could do about it.

CHAPTER 10

It was very late when Perrin finally walked home from work through the streets of Tamba, lugging the cage with two very unhappy magic sniffers.

It was so much later than he usually returned home. Ever since these problems started—with the dragon and the pumans —he'd barely come home at the usual time. Dorella had already commented on it.

Most of the businesses were closed, the windows dark. Rubbish bins stood in the street for collection in the morning.

To his surprise, Dorella was still in the shop, cleaning behind the empty shelves of the counter.

"Thank goodness, there you are," she said. She looked rather tired and relieved.

"You haven't been waiting for me, have you? I can let myself in. I've done that many times, especially this week. I was held up at work. No need to worry."

"There is a visitor for you."

Her tone of imminent importance sent a chill down Perrin's

spine. If the visitor had been important enough for her to stay here rather than go home, this couldn't be a good thing.

Who could this be?

Had it been just a few months ago, he might have thought that it was someone from the court, but the case with Atreyo's family was all settled and there was no need for anyone to contact him about it. He had just come from the Bureau, so it couldn't be anyone from work either.

Oh no, certainly this could not be about the dragon again?

He asked, "Where is this person?"

"I sent her to wait upstairs," Dorella said. "I hope you don't mind. She was making me kind of nervous being inside the shop. But she was getting very impatient when you didn't turn up. She must really want to talk to you."

Well, that sounded even more ominous.

"Do you know her?"

"She's not a customer at the shop. She's quite a lady."

"Did she say what she wanted?"

"She wouldn't talk to me at all. That sort of people usually don't. They send their staff to do the talking."

No, that did not sound good at all. Someone from his previous life. And those rich people never turned up anywhere unless they wanted something.

Perrin made sure that the jacket on his uniform was straight, and slowly walked up the stairs. Both magic sniffers made excited squeaky noises. Magic sniffers were quite smart. They recognised the smells of this place and they knew they would be fed soon.

Both of them rustled in the straw and squeaked while running from one side of the cage to the other, raising themselves on their hind legs when they came to the corner and had to turn around.

At the top of the stairs, the room opened out into a rather

pleasing high-ceilinged sitting room with a vaulted ceiling and a generous hearth where a fire roared—Dorella must have lit it— and oil lamps cast a warm glow.

His dining table sat in the middle of this space, and at the table, surrounded by the last of the paraphernalia of moving his stuff back in here and the smell of newly cut wood, was none other than Mirella Dianello, sister to Perrin's late partner Atreyo.

A high-class lady indeed, and probably his least favourite guess for who might be waiting for him.

And also, wasn't the court case over and done with, and was he supposed to not be dealing with Mirella and her entitled family anymore?

"Good afternoon," he said, because he couldn't think of saying anything else out of all the things he wanted to say, but that were not polite enough for conversation.

He couldn't see the red folder with the documents that she used to carry during the court case, but on the table in front of her stood a box such as people sent through the mail.

His mind was racing to touch on all the disasters that could be hidden within. Was this something that had arrived in Atreyo's name? That she could claim was his to deal with?

"I see you have made this place rather homely," Mirella said.

"The carpenter just finished last month."

"You're going to live here?"

"Yes. I quite like it."

"It's a tiny place above a shop." And apparently one wasn't supposed to live above a shop.

"I don't need more and I quite like it here. This floor used to be one narrow corridor with some store rooms. Dorella used to hire the rooms out."

"If one didn't know that you were not that way inclined, one might gossip about living with a single woman."

"This is a business. Dorella does not live here."

In fact, she lived across the road.

But Mirella would probably know that as well, and this was just her way to needle him about potential gossip that might arise in some circles. She was very skilled at that.

Perrin lifted the cage with the magic sniffers, and put it on the table next to the parcel that she had brought. He'd placed it deliberately in a position so that they could see Mirella and sniff her parcel. Although both were now so hungry that he didn't want to trust their judgement about magic too much.

They both ran to Mirella's side of the cage and stuck their noses through the bars.

Mirella pulled a face. "You put animals on the table?"

"Yes, I need to give these two little guys some food right now." He opened the door to one half of the cage and took Zan out. He was used to being handled and hung relaxed in Perrin's hand.

"Excuse me, I need to put them over there." He gestured at the cages along the back wall with the hand that held Zan.

The disgust on her face increased. She pushed herself a little away from the table.

In the cages along the back of the wall, his collection of magic sniffers was making little squeaky noises. Zan was one of his young ones. It had been his first day at work, and his mother Frida sat on her hind legs squeaking loudly. Perrin put him into the empty cage next to her so that they could lick each other's noses through the bars. He shook some grain into the food bowl. Then he repeated the process with Yaro.

"You have so many of these creatures," she said.

"Yes, there are eight. There will be more soon. I'm the only breeder of magic sniffers in town, and they are very fine animals indeed. I've taken a new one on his first trip just now. He will have a few more trips before I can pass him onto the bureau, or a merchant who wants one to detect magic in offered wares."

He met her eyes, because he knew that many of the aristo-cratic upper class had little magic trinkets and were nervous about this new direction that the Bureau of Magic Abuse was taking, that all citizens of Tamba should be subject to magic checking.

"But what brings you here?" He pulled a chair back, but instead of sitting on it, he leaned over the backrest with his elbows resting on top. She still sat at the table, so he was taller than her, and he was hoping he'd she'd get the message that he would not get bullied by her.

She now grabbed the parcel that she had brought.

"A few days ago, this arrived in the mail."

She pushed the parcel across the table.

It was an ordinary cardboard box, exactly the same type that was used all over the realms for mailing. The label at the front was also a very regular one that gave little away about its sender. The address, in neat script, probably written by someone from the Postal Service, said *to the estate of Atreyo Dianello.*

The parcel was quite heavy. The return address on the back was a simple mail service number and an address in Gaminia.

"Gaminia," he said, his tone flat.

"Yes, Gaminia."

Her tone betrayed that she would like to say, *That's your department.*

Gaminia was known as the whale kingdom. It consisted of many tiny islands, but the vast majority of the kingdom lay underwater, the main inhabitants being whales. As far as he knew, there were some people on those islands, and they were allowed to live there as protectors of the kingdom.

He looked at her. "What sort of interactions do you have with Gaminia?"

"None," she said in a precious voice. "It is addressed to the estate of my brother. We know nothing about his dealings with the other realms."

"I thought we agreed that I have no say in Atreyo's old business dealings. I have that in writing, signed by the judge."

She glared at him, and he glared back.

Clearly, she thought that the court-determined boundaries should not apply when events inconvenienced her.

The silence lingered. Two magic sniffers wriggled their noses at each other through the bars. They made little snuffling noises when they did this.

"I have taken this infernal parcel to all the people that I could think of who might help me solve this mystery, but they're all at a loss about what I am supposed to be doing with it."

She said all this through clenched teeth, and Perrin figured that the arrival of the parcel at her doorstep was not quite as recent as she made out, and also that she must have taken this thing all over town before she came to him, and also that she clearly had a strong incentive to deal with it.

"So then, you're bringing it to me as a last resort?"

"You know about... these things."

"Magic things?"

She nodded, once. Her lips twitched.

"Well, then, open it and let's see. I can't guarantee I can help and if it turns out I'll need to spend a significant amount of time on it, you'll have to negotiate compensation for my time with Inspector Carbin."

And he was pretty sure she would say no, because he was far too busy.

She gave him a dirty look but lifted the lid off the parcel.

In the middle of a bed of soft white sand sat a strange natural object that could only be described as a very large barnacle. Not like the tiny barnacles that grew on the pylons and walls at the quayside, but one as big as the palm of his hand.

As soon as the lid was fully off the box, the lid-like contraption in the middle of the barnacle opened and a terrible screeching sound came out. Perrin clamped his hands over his ears.

He had heard of these. They were screamers: the way the whales of Gaminia communicated with land creatures. And whales being whales, they usually communicated their displeasure.

Perrin slammed the lid of the top of the box, and the noise continued muffled for a little while, before stopping altogether.

"What does it say?" he asked.

"I don't know. No one will tell me. That's why I'm here."

"Why are you taking this to me in my private house? You should take it to the Bureau's public inquiry office during business hours. They have ways of translating screamers."

"In the *public* office downstairs," she said.

She looked at him, and he looked back, and realised that she didn't want to take this thing into the bureau, because when they translated the screamer by putting it in a tub of water, it would speak its message aloud, and the people in the room, those people waiting to hear advice about their own magical items, might hear.

"Is there anything I should know about?"

"I just don't want people listening."

Of course, there was never anything "just" about dealing with these high-class people.

Perrin made a few quick calculations.

He did not want to get involved in whatever problem she had gotten herself involved in, because he had enough problems to deal with right now, but not helping her could well mean the difference between having a decent job and getting paid well and living in poverty. Such was the influence of the rich families.

"Well, I can help you translate it. Not here and not now,

because I don't have the required objects. But if you come into the bureau tomorrow morning—"

"I would rather not."

"I understand. But that is the only way I am going to deal with it. I don't have the objects necessary."

"But I thought you'd want to do it for Atreyo. It's addressed to his estate."

"True, but I also remember the judge's ruling that I'm no longer responsible for it. I have a distinct memory of being told that not only was Atreyo's estate no longer my responsibility, I could also no longer make any claims on it. I'd denounced my claim in return for being paid out. So if I get involved, I'll be breaking that ruling and someone could take me to court for that."

He looked at her and she looked back and the unspoken moment passed between them. Of course, "someone" was likely to be the Dianello family, and he wasn't going to fall into that trap. But Mirella was probably not smart enough to have come here for that reason.

"Look, something tells me that you already know what this is likely to be about. If you really want me to help you, then you will have to tell me what is going on." He looked at her, and she looked at him, but she didn't say anything.

"Otherwise you will just have to come to the bureau and we can deal with it properly."

"Fine then," she said. She grabbed the box and put it in her handbag, then she got up from her seat and crossed the room.

Ha. If she thought this was a way to deal with the problem...

Whales sent screamers if they wanted something. She would be back. And if not... well, that wasn't his problem.

Mirella stopped at the top of the stairs and looked at him in a *well, aren't you going to say anything?* way.

He didn't. Say anything, that was.

Instead, he also got up and picked up the bag of grain to start feeding the rest of the magic sniffers.

Mirella said, "This is a screamer. It will keep getting louder and eventually we'll be able to hear it without opening the lid."

She had done some research, obviously.

"Yes."

He waited until she spoke again.

"Can I leave it with you so you can take it to the bureau?"

"Absolutely not. Screamers demand a response from whomever owns them. I have quite enough problems to deal with already."

She hesitated.

"Well... then... Could you take me to the bureau?"

"I said you can go in tomorrow mo—"

"No, now."

She had to be joking. "I have to feed the animals." And he was tired after having to deal with the dragon.

"I'll wait."

He was also hungry, but he wasn't going to give her the satisfaction of seeing him complain. Besides, he was starting to get quite curious about what could prompt Gaminia to send the family a screamer, and what the Dianello family were hiding. Because what the family did might not be his business as a magic inspector, but whatever came out of Gaminia definitely was. And as far as he remembered, the parcel might be addressed to Atreyo's estate, but Atreyo had always avoided dealing with Gaminia.

CHAPTER II

While Mirella waited at the table, Perrin collected the tin of grain and shook some in the bowl of each of the eight cages that stood on shelves against the back wall. The magic sniffers all came out of the straw to eat, including Frida, whose belly bulged on both sides of her body. It dragged over the straw.

She nosed in the grain, but returned to the straw after only nibbling at it. She preferred fruit, and the fruit would have to wait until he came back.

Then he put his cloak back on his shoulders and led Mirella down the stairs, all of it without speaking a word.

They walked through the streets in uncomfortable silence. All the shops were closed now and even the last lingering shop owners had gone home.

Perrin didn't know what to say to her, since everything he said could be used against him, and she probably felt the same way. After the court case, where the family had chosen to pay him out for work rendered to Atreyo's business rather than have him go after Atreyo's house, he and the family had parted ways without speaking to each other, and they had avoided him in the time since.

She had to be really desperate to come to him for help.

They arrived at the Bureau's office. The stately two-storey building with its carved sandstone cornices depicting all kinds of creatures, from trolls to whales and dragons, looked rather menacing in the darkness. A set of solid marble steps led up to the ornately carved wooden doors—stained black with oil—with little oval windows to either side.

The doors were normally open, but at this time of day, Perrin needed to use the key he always carried.

The lock was stiff, and the door creaked.

Their footsteps echoed in the hall, and the thud of the shutting door almost sounded like a prison door clanging shut.

For after-hours visitors, a large book lay open on a table just inside the hall. By the golden glow of a flapping oil light, Perrin read that someone had come in after hours two days ago *to replace the door to my magic sniffer cage* from the workshop at the back of the building.

Perrin took the pencil and wrote *to test a parcel of gifts* and signed it with his name. He wasn't sure if people were later questioned about this and if he would have to explain his visit in more detail.

The magic inspectors and their open office upstairs formed only part of the Bureau of Magic Abuse's services. Other than the investigators across the hall, the building also housed inspectors that looked at the trains and ones that inspected the mail. These occupied rooms on the ground floor of the building, and there was a fairly recent addition: a public office where members of the public could bring in goods and parcels they received for testing.

This was a stately old-fashioned room with black-and-white checkered tiles on the floor, dark wooden benches, ornate light sconces and a heavy wooden counter on one end, divided into four cubicles where inspectors would see people.

This part of the building was now dark, lit by the sputtering light of a few lights burning low on oil. Perrin had to fill a few reservoirs to make sure that they weren't plunged into darkness.

Behind the counter sat a long table with the equipment the regular workers in this office used to detect magic. There would normally also be a cage with magic sniffers, but at night the caretaker took them to the animal house in the courtyard.

Perrin needed to unlock the gate that allowed employees access to this part of the room, and then had to light another lamp so that he could see where the contraption he needed stood.

Mirella remained in the middle of the room, clamping her arms around herself.

"I don't understand how you can work in this place," she said. "It gives me the creeps."

"It's quite busy here during the day."

Whenever he had come here, there were always plenty of people waiting to be seen by the magic testers. The room had been a suggestion from Inspector Carbin and the Bureau considered it a great success.

He walked along the bench tightly packed with all kinds of devices, holding aloft the light and studying all the strange contraptions.

There was a sniff-box, where you could enclose a parcel in a chamber, pump in air with a bellows on the side and let the air out through a valve which blew it over a piece of paper—that you had to soak in a special solution—which turned yellow if it detected magic.

It only detected types of illusion magic common to the realm of Validor. Magic sniffers were not much use for that sort of magic.

Another contraption was a set of silver scales. It came with an ornately carved box that contained a special set of weights made from ironstone. During the demonstration for all the inspectors, Inspector Carbin had used these scales to weigh a simple glass jar, which, despite being empty, weighed more than it would have when filled with rocks. When she poured water in the jar, it turned green. Pouring the liquid through another device with a funnel, tubes and glass chambers with gemstones then identified the green water as the highly illegal dragons' tears, a potion that dulled the senses. Incidentally, it had nothing to do with dragons.

At the end of the bench, Perrin found the contraption he had come to use: a big and heavy basin carved from marble with carvings of runes on the outside. A heavy wooden lid covered the top. Perrin had to use all his strength to push it aside.

The water inside was dark and oily. It smelled of seawater, salty and earthy, because it was sea water, from the whale kingdom of Gaminia. A chain made from whale bones was attached to a knob in a recess along the top and when Perrin hauled it up, it brought up a basket, also made of whale bones.

The recess in the top also held a box in which lived a couple of clam shells. One needed to use a pair of whalebone tongs to pick one out of the water—they tended to slam shut their shells when they got spooked and having one's finger caught was not a nice experience.

Perrin asked Mirella for the box with the screamer.

He couldn't take it out of the box without opening the lid, of course, so he had to clench his teeth while the screamer wailed its screeching message.

The instructions said to wear gloves, but he didn't have any, so he used the sleeves of his jacket to pick it up.

Screamers could bite, he knew.

He took great pleasure in seeing Mirella in the corner of the room with her hands over her ears, looking very distressed.

He deposited the thing into the basket, then loosened the chain and dropped the basket into the water so that the screamer was just covered.

At least the noise was reduced to low keening when it hit the water.

Then he took the whalebone tongs, picked up a clam and dropped it into the basket as well.

Then he lowered the basket until it vanished into the dark depths of the basin.

The wailing became even softer.

A few bubbles rose to the surface.

And then, slowly, the wail morphed into a different sound. First bursts of noise like the barking of a dog. Then those bursts of sound transformed into audible words that repeated and became clearer until Perrin could understand them.

"Return to the kingdom that which belongs to the kings. Return the possessions of the school what belongs to them. This is the last warning. Further disobedience will incur the wrath of the kingdom. Our wrath will be revengeful and terrible."

Perrin grabbed a piece of paper and wrote down the words.

It repeated this until Perrin pulled the chain up, the water ran out of the basket and it started screaming again.

Perrin picked the screamer up, dropped it into its box and shut the lid.

Phew. Silence.

Then he looked at Mirella and read what he had written.

"What does it mean?" she asked, her eyes wide.

"You have something that Gaminia considers theirs and they want it back."

She snorted. "Well... well, I wouldn't know what's in all the stuff that came from Atreyo's business. Why doesn't it tell us what sort of thing this is?"

"That's Gaminia for you. Whales are not simple to deal with. They rarely talk to anyone directly and when they do communicate, they're always very vague. You cannot ask them questions because they won't reply, and they never explain anything."

"So, what am I supposed to do with this?" She gestured at the box.

"The whales are very peculiar about possessions," Perrin said. "They don't have many, but those possessions they do have are treasured and have mythical properties. They would never ask for anything to be returned if it wasn't important to them."

"It would be handy if they said what it was."

"That's what the whales are like. Do you have anything that came from the ocean? Shells, fish bones, parts of a ship wreckage?"

She shook her head. "We don't have anything like that. Things at the bottom of the ocean get disgusting, with barnacles all over them. I wouldn't keep that in the house. We don't have anything to do with whales. You can't talk to them. They just do whatever they want while they're living in the ocean. It must be a mistake."

"Whales don't make mistakes. They have senses that we don't have and know many things that we don't understand."

She shrugged. "Well, we have Atreyo's collection and this is addressed to him."

He looked at her and she looked back at him, knowing that neither of them knew what was in Atreyo's vast collection of magical trinkets and devices.

"So, if I were you, I would go through everything in the collection to see if you can find an object that looks like it might belong to Gaminia."

"Can't you do it?"

"It's not my stuff anymore."

Another silence.

"But I wouldn't know how to tell. Also, he's been dead two years now, and he's had these items for many more years. Gaminia could have asked for whatever it is before this time, rather than bothering us with it."

"They could have, but they're whales and whales do whatever whales want."

"Supposing… I found it, what would I need to do?"

"Depending on what it is, you could give it to us and the Bureau will make sure it's returned, or you could send it, or…"

He stopped. No, he'd best not say any more.

"Or what?"

"It really depends on what the object is and how it came to be in your family's possession…"

"But you would know that, right? Having lived with Atreyo?"

"Not necessarily. I don't remember having seen anything from Gaminia. Atreyo didn't like dealing with whales because whales can be so slow and unpredictable, and they never say clearly what they want."

"But I wouldn't know where to begin."

She looked genuinely helpless, and Perrin felt a seed of pity for her. Only a little bit, though. But the wrath of Gaminia could be a terrible thing.

Every child in Tamba learned about Captain Fiddlestick and his boat, who disappeared after trying to outrun angry whales.

He sighed. "I guess I could help you a bit, in the time I have available after work, but I would need to be compensated for it."

Her face hardened. "Of course there would be money involved."

Perrin left any potential replies to this sting, such as *well, you have plenty* or *do you think the rent pays itself?* hang between them.

"Well, either I help, or I don't. It's all the same to me." He picked up the box and handed it back to her. She didn't want to take it back.

"Can't it stay here?"

"Absolutely not. The screamer is the problem that belongs to those it's been sent to. The Bureau will have no responsibility for the problems of your family. We even agreed about that in court."

She looked disappointed and at that moment, Perrin knew that she hadn't been looking to solve the problem, she had been looking for someone to take the problem off her hands. And he wasn't going to give her that satisfaction.

"I can't help you any further, because I would need to go through all of Atreyo's collections to see what he could possibly have that might trigger this request. I will need some time to do this, and I have a job, so either you go officially through the Bureau, or I will do it for you in my time after work, when I have time, which won't be soon, and I'll need to be paid for it."

She looked at him. Her mouth twitched.

After a while, she said, "All right then. Not the Bureau. I don't want them involved. Come to the house tomorrow." But her words sounded like they were spoken through clenched teeth.

CHAPTER 12

But Perrin didn't get much time to think about Mirella or her screamer.

When he came back home, he found Frida in her nest in the company of seven little pink jellybeans. Some of them were still wet and by the way her belly shivered and she licked her backside, he thought there might be more to come.

He left her to it and cut up fruit for the other magic sniffers and cleaned out the cages. When he finally returned to Frida, she had produced two more tiny pink, semi-transparent lumps. They were small enough to fit on the tip of his finger. Their tails were tiny, their eyes still shut, their incoherently waving paws soft. Most of them had latched onto Frida's nipples, and Perrin pushed the last one over until it was also feeding. Then he skewered pieces of fruit onto a stick and fed them to Frida.

He should really start thinking more seriously about selling his previous brood.

Perrin spent the next day at work trying to find someone to take the dragon back to Solania.

The owner of the warehouse was not happy about the

dragon. He might be used to housing animals, he said, but this dragon was just ill-behaved.

The boy who looked after it told him that whenever he opened the cage, the dragon would spray piss through the bars and work dung out between the bars.

"It's handy because I haven't had to use the rakes, but the creature stinks up the whole warehouse. It should be doing its business in a corner of the cage where we can clean it, but it has been spraying piss all over the place, even out the window. It won't let anyone clean the cage anymore. It got hold of a couple of horsehair blankets that we use to put in between furniture inside the carriages and we can't get them back. They're in the cage with the straw."

Perrin went to have a look. The dragon's eye appeared behind the tiny window.

Was he imagining it or had the orange iris become more flecked with gold?

Something was changing about the dragon. It was maturing.

When he got to work, he went to see Inspector Carbin, who sat at her desk, an expression of thunder on her face.

"Yes," she said when he came in.

Oh dear, not a good time.

"About the dragon…"

"What about it?"

"It needs to be moved."

"Yes, tell me something new."

"In a hurry."

"You were working on that, weren't you?"

"It's not easy. I may need to hire a boat."

Now she looked up. The expression on her face was one of incredulity. "A boat?"

"Yes."

"Just like that?"

They looked at each other for a while, and then she started laughing.

"A boat? A whole boat? Big enough to carry the dragon?"

"Why is that funny?"

"Because we don't have the budget! And we know nothing about boats, and have nothing to do with boats, and most boat owners and captains and their crew don't like us one bit."

"We may not have another option." He suspected that the dislike was mutual.

"There is always another option, Dear Perrin, you have been hoodwinked by people who sell boats."

"There is no way for me to move the dragon if I can't put it on a boat and I can't put it on the train and trucks won't carry it."

"Who told you those things?"

"Everyone. Parvo."

"Yes, he would say that, but when it really comes to it, they will change their minds."

Perrin shook his head.

"Not at all?"

"Nope. That's why I want a boat."

"That's ridiculous. We don't have money for a boat. Let me go and talk to the railway people. They can't just refuse paying customers."

She got up from her desk, and swept all the papers in a heap. "I'll be glad if I don't have to think about this mess for a while."

Good, because that feeling was mutual. If she could bully Parvo into taking the dragon, then that was all the better.

He started filing his inspection reports. He might actually be able to finish on time today—and then he realised he'd forgotten about visiting Mirella after work.

Well, he'd just take a quick look at Atreyo's stuff, find nothing—because there was nothing there—and then he'd be able to leave again.

Inspector Carbin, however, came back quicker than he had expected. If she'd been angry before, that was nothing compared to how angry she looked now. Her face was red and glistened with sweat. Her normally immaculate jacket hung askew on her shoulders.

"He won't budge," she said. "I asked him what else he expects us to do with a dragon and he said it was my problem. He was quite rude about it, too."

Another inspector asked, "What's that horrible smell?"

Perrin knew exactly what the smell was.

"My shoe was the only thing that got wet," she said. She looked at Perrin. "That animal has to go."

"Yes. I told you."

She met his eyes as if for the first time truly understanding him.

Then she took in a deep breath. "I'll see if I can make something happen."

Then when he finished work, he had to look at Atreyo's collection. This was held in the house of Atreyo's parents who, according to Mirella, were travelling in the country. To get to the house, he had to walk past Mirella's house, which was the house where he used to live with Atreyo. There were so many memories attached to this house that he had avoided even walking past the street for the past two years.

He glanced in through the window.

Mirella had moved a lot of the furniture. Atreyo abhorred houses that were cluttered and full of useless knickknacks, but Mirella loved big pieces of furniture—the more the better—and she possessed hundreds—no, thousands—or knickknacks. Atreyo had often complained that his sister had no sense of style, that her tendency to collect things that were shiny just for the sake of it made her house look cheap.

The beautiful living room was full of opulent couches that

were really too big for it. The wall was full of paintings of all different styles that didn't go together. Atreyo would turn in his grave if he knew about this.

Their parents' house was a bit further down the street.

Mirella came to the door when he knocked.

They walked through the deserted corridor.

The library was still pretty much in the same state as he had found it during his last visit, now almost a year ago. The family didn't appear to be using this room very much other than as a place to store boxes of stuff they didn't need.

Of course, looking at the collection took more time than he planned.

Perrin spent most of the evening going through boxes of items that brought back painful memories for him. He'd been through these before, and pretty much already knew that there was nothing in it that the whales would want.

Atreyo was very wary of the whale kingdom, because of some previous interaction that happened before Perrin came into the picture.

Most of Atreyo's beautiful items were still packed in the boxes where Perrin had also seen them during his last visit.

He managed to pick up a few more interesting books, because Mirella and her family cared little for those, and he argued that he could use them at the bureau.

Mirella waited on the very dusty couch that used to stand in front of the window in Atreyo's office.

It was too small for two people to sit comfortably next to each other, and it was called a lovers' seat, because you had to squeeze in next to each other.

He and Atreyo used to sit there sometimes and reminisce about the good times or to look at a box of samples that Atreyo had been sent. Perrin could still smell the sharpness of the exotic spices.

Perrin got to the end of the boxes from Atreyo's office. A few remaining items stood to the side, but Perrin didn't remember having seen them before.

"Is this also part of the collection?" he asked.

"Everything to do with my brother's business is kept in this room," Mirella said.

She was looking at the door, because children's voices sounded in the hallway. Perrin guessed these were her kids and by the sound of things, they were getting into a fight.

"I haven't found anything yet. Can I look in these boxes? This doesn't look familiar."

"Go ahead. I'm sorry, but you'll have to excuse me. I have to go and see what the kids are up to. I told them to stay home."

She got up from her seat and left the room.

Perrin opened the lid of the box on top of the pile.

On a bed of velvet inside lay a set of tableware. The knives and forks, spoons and serving tongs were made from silver with ornate handles with little embedded jewels.

Atreyo used to say that a classy style was characterised by its deceptive simplicity. You did not paint intricate plates with complicated patterns. Too much colour would detract from the artistry of the porcelain. Similarly, if you were going to create artistry in silversmithing, you did not embed coloured stones, because it resulted in a garish ensemble.

This tableware set was super-garish.

There was no way in the world that Atreyo would ever have allowed something like this inside his home. He would call this an ugly abomination.

Perrin was about to close the lid again when he noticed a piece of paper underneath the serving spoons.

An invoice, to be precise, made out to Mr Roban Dianello—Atreyo's older brother.

He paid—what?—for this tasteless kitsch? Why? What did

he know about fine art and antiques? He dealt in stone and marble.

Mirella's and the children's voices sounded in the hallway.

"No, I told you to stay home and do your work," Mirella said.

A child cried.

Perrin closed the box, put it aside and opened the next box on the pile.

It contained a set of gold-rimmed plates with carved crystal glasses. There were only five plates—a full set was eight and Atreyo would never buy a set unless it was complete—and they were similarly garish, with paintings of pink roses.

The next box contained a set of carafes that looked like they were made of coloured crystal, but Perrin recognised the signs of fakery. These were simple painted glass.

He didn't understand what this junk was doing here, as part of Atreyo's collections. Atreyo would never have bought these things.

He lifted a glass cup out. The merest twinkle of light dancing around the rim indicated magic.

This glass probably came from Validor and would have looked great over there, but anything that came from Validor was shrouded in illusion magic. The merchants of Validor were the greatest con artists in all the realms.

Illusion magic ran out after a while.

Urgh. He put the thing back and shut the box.

Then Mirella came back into the room.

"I'm sorry about that," she said. "Those kids, you know..." She spread her hands.

Perrin didn't know because he didn't have kids.

"Have you found anything?" she then asked.

"No, and I think I'm done, because these boxes don't belong to Atreyo's collection." He gestured at the pile he'd just looked at.

"Oh, I'm sorry. I'm pretty sure they're part of the business. My brother comes to store stuff in here every now and then."

"Your brother?"

Perrin didn't know Atreyo's older brother very well. During much of the time that he had lived with Atreyo, their oldest brother had lived as administrator in the country and he would only come on special holidays. Then he remembered the invoice.

"Yes, he has been continuing Atreyo's business."

"Wait. You mean importing and exporting?"

"Yes. As far as I know. He says we shouldn't let the business die."

"Why didn't you say anything about that before?"

"I thought you knew."

She met his eyes and a few months' worth of uncomfortable, civilised, but under-the-surface hostile interactions passed between them.

He could say that he'd been too busy fending off the family's legal attacks on his very existence to notice peripheral stuff like this, but he chose to keep the visit amicable. Because clearly, the family was desperate for help, or maybe only Mirella was, but Perrin was curious. Most of the court case had been run by Atreyo's father and neither Mirella nor her brother Roban had much to do with the proceedings.

So he said, "Well, I didn't know."

"I'm so sorry. Yes, my brother has been trying to keep Atreyo's business alive. It seems a pity after he has spent so much time setting it up to just let it die. Roban already has other businesses that import goods, so it seems natural."

"And these boxes belong to him?"

"It could be. If you're sure these didn't belong to Atreyo."

"I'm sure. And he has continued importing fine goods from the realms under Atreyo's name?"

"As far as I know, yes. He does have the same family name."

"Then what's to say that this letter addressed to Atreyo's estate is actually about any of the stuff that's here, because I can't see anything in Atreyo's old stuff that would trigger anger from Gaminia, and I know for fact that Atreyo was very careful in dealing with Gaminia, because of his past experience."

Not only that, but Mirella would know about that past experience, because Atreyo had been quite young and still living with his parents.

In the uncomfortable silence that followed, Mirella averted her eyes and looked at the floor.

"This isn't about Atreyo's business, is it?" Perrin asked.

"Honestly, I didn't know where else to turn or who to ask, and Roban just refuses to deal with it."

"So you know what it's about?"

"Sort of. Not quite. But it's tearing him apart, and he refuses to go to the authorities."

"Why me?"

"Because you know about magic stuff. And because..." Her face twitched. She pressed her lips together to stop them shaking. "I miss Atreyo. He was so much fun. And you were always part of the action. I thought you might want to... I don't know. I'd pay you if I can. It's not about the stupid money. Roban needs help. I was hoping you'd find something, but... I didn't know what else to do."

CHAPTER 13

It was very late, Perrin needed to go home to look after the magic sniffers, and Mirella had to look after the children, so he agreed to meet her the next morning, away from the house.

Perrin suggested Dorella's tea room. She agreed, even if, or maybe because, it wasn't a place where she would normally come.

She didn't want to be seen, especially not by her family.

Perrin went home with more questions than answers.

Why hadn't she told him directly that it wasn't about Atreyo's things? Why had she wasted his time sitting there and watching him go through all of it?

When he came home, the magic sniffers were all running around in their cages, even Frida. He was glad to see this, because mothers could lose a lot of weight after they had young.

He cut up the fruit and cleaned the cages, refreshed the water and the straw and then he could finally look after himself.

His mind was buzzing so much with the different possibilities of trouble that Atreyo's family could have gotten themselves in that he'd almost forgotten about his own, very large, dragon-shaped problem.

But through the combination of unusual circumstances, an idea was starting to form in the back of his mind, and thinking about it kept him awake.

That and the scufflings of the magic sniffers in their cages. He checked on Frida and the young a few times, but they were all fast asleep.

Perrin went to meet Mirella in the tea room the next morning. He thought he was early, but when he came down, Mirella was already there.

She was the only customer in the room and she sat at the table furthest in the corner, eying Dorella who was behind the counter laying out fresh pastries that the boy had brought in from the woman who baked them for her. Dorella eyed Mirella in turn and Perrin felt like he had just walked into something. Was it such a good idea to meet Mirella here? Usually, a few regulars turned up for breakfast. He just hadn't expected Mirella to be so early.

He asked Dorella to bring tea and a plate with a selection of sweet and savoury mini-buns and joined Mirella at the table.

"You're early."

She met his eyes and in them he saw a deep unease and fear, something that he hadn't seen the previous night. His attempt at being light-hearted fell flat.

"Anything wrong?"

"Yes, I don't have much time. My husband doesn't know I'm here and I need to look after the kids. Someone broke into my brother's house last night and made a mess of the place. We're still trying to find out if they stole anything, but they left a threatening message to our family."

"I'm not the right person to see about that. That's serious. You should take it to the guards."

She didn't react to that. She pressed her lips together.

"The guards can't help us. The threats are coming from outside the realms."

"How do you know? Was it a magical message?"

She nodded, once, without meeting his eyes.

He guessed: another screamer? A ransom letter that attached itself to the hands of the person who opened it? A letter that had a built-in threat like it would explode, cause a fire, or start yelling embarrassing facts? With magic from all the realms effective in Tamba, the possibilities were endless.

"And this is related to the screamer you brought in for me to translate? You know more than you've told me, right?"

Now her eyes glistened. "Please, help me. I'm scared. You're the only one I can talk to about this. My brother just won't listen. He's destroying himself. He's destroying us, as a family."

Dorella came to bring a tray with tea and buns, and they were silent while she set the things on the table. Dorella met Perrin's eyes. They were pretty good looking out for each other these days. Her intense look seemed to ask if he was all right. He nodded ever so slightly. If anything, this conversation was only uncomfortable for Mirella.

"Have some sweet buns," Perrin said.

"Thank you, but I've already had breakfast."

Another silence lingered while Perrin helped himself.

"If you really want me to help you, I simply cannot do anything further than what I've already done without knowing the truth. So if you want my help, you'll have to tell me more."

At first she said nothing, and Perrin was going to suggest they were wasting time. He was annoyed about that. He wanted to enjoy Dorella's pastries.

But then she started, "About a month ago, my brother received a shipment of goods from the realms that's ruffled some feathers. There were a number of boxes, mostly filled with junk as far as I could see."

"Wait, those were the extra boxes that were supposedly part of Atreyo's collection that you got me to look at, right?"

She nodded. "I hoped that you would see something unusual in them."

"That stuff was junk. Not remotely of the quality that Atreyo would have been interested in."

She looked at her hands. "He kept most of the other stuff in his office. He won't tell me what else is in the shipment, but after yesterday, I'm sure it contains this thing Gaminia is asking for. I don't know what it is. I genuinely don't know. I don't know where my brother got the shipment, but he doesn't want the authorities involved, which can't mean anything good."

"Nope."

"I know my brother wanted to invest in quality collectors' items, and I've heard him say that he doesn't want to sell them within Tamba—"

"Because magic is illegal here."

She looked down. "He wanted to sell the things in other realms."

"So, where did he get this collection?"

"Apparently some old wizard died, and he'd collected all these things that had to be sold."

"What does your brother know about magic?"

She shrugged.

Not much, Perrin guessed.

"His business is with special building materials. Marble and black granite and things like that."

"Why did he buy this collection, then?"

"As I said, he wanted to continue Atreyo's business. Because he's... our brother, you know?"

In Perrin's experience, rich people never did things out of the goodness of their hearts. Not these sorts of things, at least. This had to be because he'd thought he could make money. Maybe he'd been offered something he'd judged too good to refuse, only to discover that he should have refused it.

"Is there a chance I could get to see this collection? The important parts, not the dregs that he doesn't want, either."

Mirella shrugged. "He doesn't want any of the authorities involved. He doesn't know I'm talking to you."

"But your house is being broken into and your family is being threatened."

She shrugged again.

After having initially rejected any of the food, she now grabbed a pastry and sipped from her tea. Perrin felt sorry for her, but he also didn't want to get too involved because this really was a matter for the Bureau and Inspector Carbin would not be impressed if he went off on his own and investigated.

But if the Dianello family was not happy to make a formal complaint—and all the signs were that they wouldn't—then there was nothing the Bureau could do. Maybe things needed to get worse before they got better.

He wasn't sure how much effort and risk he was willing to take for the sake of a family that had treated him as a second-rank citizen for most of the time he'd been with Atreyo.

And he was definitely not going to sneak into Atreyo's brother's office without his consent. But Roban had sway over something Perrin could use.

He left Mirella with some homework: questions to answer about the nature of the shipment, where it had come from, who had sold it. If she was concerned, maybe she should do the work. Until such time that something blew up and she had to go to the Bureau after all.

He needed to go to work now, so after seeing Mirella off, he ran upstairs, grabbed two magic sniffers from his growing collection, dressed in his uniform and walked to the Bureau.

The table with the large book to sign in only stood in the hall at night. He wondered if anyone had looked at it yet and wondered why he'd visited at night.

Upstairs in the large room, no unpleasant surprises waited for him, thank goodness. Perrin collected his list of venues to be inspected off the table. The list was quite short, because it also contained the message, *the mayor wants to discuss the dragon.*

Sure, the mayor wanted that.

But Perrin duly went to see the mayor in his office in the town square, with the plush seats that made him think that if he sat down, he would fall asleep.

The mayor had heard about the dragon.

He said, in his usual self-important tone, "I wanted to speak to you because I've been thinking."

Thinking and Tarlo Firello were two things that didn't always go together well.

"Since you have so much trouble returning the dragon to Solania, how about we just... keep it here?"

Perrin almost spat out his tea. "Excuse, Mayor, did you say *keep it here?*"

"You heard me well enough the first time, but yes, that's what I said. If we could keep it in a large cage or some such, we could turn it into an attraction, you know, for the children of Tamba. They don't get to see magical creatures often."

"Oh, I... am not sure if that is such a good idea."

It was a *very bad* idea, he was sure of that. One dragon attracted other dragons, because they were known to roam over large distances. And if visitors from other realms saw that Tamba kept a dragon, they would, rightfully, question Tamba's commitment to keeping magic out. A dragon was a magical creature, after all.

And that was on top of the challenges of containing the dragon while it grew. And who was going to be burdened with the burden that was the dragon? Not the mayor, that was for sure.

"No," Perrin said. "As an officer of the Bureau of Magic Abuse, I say no. I will see to it that it's returned to Solania. In fact, I was wondering if the council has any boats available."

Tarlo Firello laughed. "What? You want to use our ferries to take a dragon all the way to Solania? They are made out of wood. One breath from the creature and that's bye, bye boat."

"If it eats only vegetable matter, it won't breathe fire."

"I heard it had no issue breathing fire in the past few days."

"That's because it's been eating rats."

"Ha ha, tell me another story. No, you are clearly being obstinate. I will go to your boss myself and propose that we set up a permanent enclosure for the beast."

And Inspector Carbin—being funded by the mayor—would have no option but to listen to the harebrained plan. Heavens, she might even want to go along with it for her own reasons.

That wouldn't end well.

CHAPTER 14

During the rest of the day, Perrin did his inspections and then made another tour of the warehouses, but no matter how much he pleaded, he found no one to transport a dragon.

Well, he was really stuck in a corner with this beast, because no one wanted it, but no one wanted to help him move the beast back to where it belonged either. And the longer he waited, the more attractive the mayor's idea of keeping the beast in a zoo would seem to some people, and, knowing the dragon as well as he did, he was absolutely sure that wouldn't end well.

He could wait until Grandmaster Yorick of Solania finally took an interest in the creature that was legally his, but Perrin suspected that he was beneath that man's attention and Solania had rather too many dragons already and they didn't feel particularly worried that one of them was creating havoc elsewhere.

The dragon was quite literally his problem, and he suspected he would need to employ some trickery to get it out of the city.

On his way out of the building in the afternoon, Verbena

came to him. He smiled at her. He kind of missed working with Verbena as he had during the dressmakers' fair.

She said, "You look miserable. Is everything all right?"

"Work is hard," he said.

"Tell me about it. And trying to work while there is so much going on at home."

Perrin was hesitant to ask further.

Verbena was a nice kid, who didn't deserve her recklessly living sister.

Apparently, the latest man and father of impending child number eight had tried to kick Verbena out of the house.

And Verbena demanded that he leave or she would leave and take the older children. Perrin heard there had been a huge fight on the street before the eyes of all. It was all such a sordid story that he felt uncomfortable asking about it, even if she didn't appear to feel embarrassed. The Verbena who lived with her sister in the harbour district was so different from the one he knew at the Bureau.

While they walked down the stairs, Verbena again asked why he was so miserable.

"I'm still dealing with that dragon," Perrin said.

"Still?" she laughed. "I thought you put it on the train?"

"Yes, and it half destroyed the carriage and frightened the workers, so they refused to carry it any further."

"Just like the truck?"

"Yes, sadly."

"But how are you going to return it to Solania?"

"That is the big question, isn't it? The trucks won't carry it. It's too big for a truck now anyway, and the trains won't carry it."

"How about you just let it go? It might find its own way back."

"Dragons are loyal to the place where they grew up. This one hatched from an egg in the warehouse at the back of the meat works."

"Oh." She frowned. "Don't your books have any suggestions?"

She meant Atreyo's books of magic. The ones he'd gone to retrieve from Mirella's house when the previous, illegal, owner of the dragon had tried selling dragon meat in her inn.

He blew out a breath. "They're magic books. They never talk about how to get rid of magic, only how to use it. The books say nothing about how to transport dragons. Those texts just assume that dragons are free creatures roaming the sky, capable of transporting themselves."

"Don't you always tell the new inspectors to read about everything?" She smiled.

There was a lot of information in those books, and unless you knew specifically what you were looking for, it was hard to find anything. But maybe it was time to look at the books again for inspiration.

For one, he might find something to control a dragon now that it was too big and powerful to be controlled by the thunder-staff. And one that was developing a nesting instinct.

"Oh well, I'll see you tomorrow," he said.

Verbena had far too many pressing problems to bother her with his problems.

He made his way home, halfway expecting Mirella to have turned up again, but she hadn't, and Dorella was still busy with a couple of customers, packing up a box of pastries. Apparently, there was some kind of festivity going on with the family.

Perrin normally spent this time chatting to Dorella. It was a time of day he enjoyed and looked forward to, but obviously, that wasn't going to happen today, so he trudged up the stairs where he returned the magic sniffers to their cages and fed the animals.

Then he cut some bread for himself, listening out for Dorella's voice to call him downstairs, but she was still talking to people.

He took Atreyo's books off the shelf. One was a book of magic foodstuffs and household items. He didn't think he'd find much in there, so he set it aside for the time being.

He took another book off the shelf, this one an old volume that Atreyo had bought secondhand. He only did that with valuable books, and this was a beautiful book about magical locations.

Not terribly useful in his current predicament, but the book had once belonged to the witch Sabyna, a wise old woman whom Atreyo would see sometimes.

Was she still alive?

She lived on the outskirts of Tamba and was a well-known figure in some groups, even if the rich rarely spoke of her, because she wasn't *one of them*, and her loyalties were murky at best. But if she had died, he was sure he would have heard about it.

He leafed through the book and got distracted by a section about Gaminia, the whale kingdom ruled by an ancient whale king. They considered the water on the surface part of their territory and would require permits from ships wanting to cross.

At work, he had checked harbour shipping movements, and spotted the name Roban Dianello on one of the documents.

If Perrin could get Roban to lend him a boat, or pay for the use of a boat, because he was pretty sure Roban didn't *own* any boats, Gaminia was more or less on the way to Solania. So if Mirella found the artefact that Gaminia wanted, he could return it... in exchange for use of the boat, and oh, I'm going to make a detour to Solania to return this dragon.

There were footsteps on the stairs.

"Do you still want your tea?" Dorella asked.

"Yes, thank you."

She had brought a tray with two cups and set it down on the table. She nodded at the books.

"What are you reading?" She looked over his shoulder. "About Gaminia?"

Perrin explained in a few sentences why Mirella had come to see him.

"You are too kind," she said, offering him a biscuit. "After everything they put you through, I would not give them any time."

"Normally I wouldn't, either, but I've always found it beneficial to keep talking to people. You never know what you will find out. She must have been extremely desperate to come to me and I was curious. Besides, it is something I do know something about, and as things stand, I can possibly turn this situation to my advantage."

She chuckled. "It looks like you're planning something."

"Not yet, just thinking about the possibilities."

"You said this screamer message she got comes from the whales. They're often very tricky creatures. How do you know that they mean what they say?"

"That's always a question with Gaminia, but screamers are considered to be quite truthful because it's very hard to imbue them with the message, so it's not something that just happens along the way."

"Gaminia would send agents along with the message and personally deliver it, if it's really that important."

He gave her a sharp look. "It sounds like you're familiar with Gaminia."

"Not really, but when I was much younger, there used to be a business nextdoor selling fancy dresses and trinkets that came from Gaminia."

"Nott's Flotsam and Jetsam." Perrin remembered hearing the business' name.

She nodded. "Exactly. Did you ever buy stuff there?"

"No, it was gone before I came to Tamba, but everyone was still talking about it."

"Yes, that's the one. Nott's son fancied me for a bit and he told me about all the things his father had to go through in order to bring in these things from Gaminia. Do you know that any ship that crosses the surface of their ocean has to apply for permission?"

"I do."

"And do you know that only certain people can act as translators? They can translate and repeat what the whales say, but they can't translate anything back, not because they couldn't translate words into whale language, but because the whales don't want to hear it. It's said they don't have ears, but that's ridiculous. Of course, the whales have ears. They're simply not interested in what we have to say to them."

"I haven't heard anyone put it to me in that way." But it was true. The whales never listened.

"That's what old Nott told me. I remember it very well, because I was so excited about his son and that our relationship might work, but then he got sent away to learn about magic and I'm just... simple Dorella in Tamba, where magic is prohibited."

"I'm sorry."

"Don't be."

"You could have gone with him."

"Yes, but I would have had to sell my business I spent so much time setting up. What if I hated it over there?"

And that, ultimately, was Dorella. Practical through and through.

"So that's the sad story about why I know a bit about Gaminia."

"Was Nott getting most of his stuff from over there?"

"As far as I know, yes. He was always complaining that it was so hard to understand what the whales meant."

"How did he even conduct trade with them?"

"There are registered sellers, who are allowed to deal with the kingdom, but they would often be called back for strange instructions that something suddenly could or could not be sold. One day, they would be happy to sell stuff made from seaweed, but the next day, it might be a different story because some current had decreed that seaweed was holy or something like that."

Seaweed, of course, was used to create thin, semi-transparent and very flexible material that the expensive dressmakers loved to incorporate in their designs.

"How did he deal with the constant changes in rules?"

"He used to say that he didn't go looking for trouble when trouble didn't come looking for him. He said that usually when a change of rule came through, he argued back, and because whales are such poor talkers, they'd often give up. He wouldn't order the object in question for a while, until he felt it was safe, but he also wouldn't stop selling his existing stock. Funnily enough, whales are very peculiar about money. For all they claim to not understand people on the land, they sure understand money."

"But you can't do anything with money under water."

"How do you know? Have you ever lived under water?"

They both laughed.

Then Dorella continued, "But kidding aside, money can buy you lots of things: ships to patrol your borders, people who will further your business interests, and people who get you the things that are really valuable to you."

"Like heirlooms."

And while he said that, something occurred to him that he hadn't thought of before. The puman people were debt collectors. Debt didn't necessarily involve money. It could also involve possessions.

The pumans had come to the old secondhand shop to look for secondhand stuff, presumably looking for particular items. A lady had come into the shop trying to sell an old trumpet that couldn't possibly work and had no clear value. He even said it looked like it had been at the bottom of the harbour for years.

Well, damn it.

What if... just if... all events from the last few days were related? If that trumpet was the thing the pumans wanted and it belonged to Gaminia. And the trumpet... was in the collection Roban Dianello had bought, which meant that the pumans were making threats to the Dianello family, because they'd been hired by Gaminia to retrieve the trumpet?

Dorella had stayed rather longer than usual, and when she left, Perrin didn't feel like going back to the books. He needed to know about this collection without asking Roban or Mirella—because they'd already shown that they'd lie to him.

But he might just have stumbled upon someone else he could ask about it.

CHAPTER 15

Mirella withheld information about her brother's actions. Perrin was sure of that.

Because if there had been a random magical attack on a well-off family, the Bureau would have been the first to have heard about it. The fact that no report had been filed with the Bureau meant that the Dianello family knew what it was about, and that it was something illegal.

But if Perrin was right, and the events were all connected, then the presence of pumans in town and the fact that someone owned a thing that was of value to Gaminia, meant there was serious trouble ahead.

And the fact that Mirella contacted him, of all people, about it showed the level of desperation they had reached. But Mirella wasn't going to tell him what was going on for fear of her brother finding out, or fear of incriminating herself, or both.

And since Mirella wouldn't talk to him, he would have to do his own investigations. Away from the Bureau, at least initially, because this was above his paygrade. If she knew about it,

Inspector Carbin would take him off the case and give it to the investigators who would not only be too slow in working on it, they would rob Perrin of his chance to get rid of his dragon.

It so happened that Atreyo's old book had reminded him of a person from his previous life who could be useful. He could ask her for an unbiased opinion whether anything untoward had happened in the sheltered, exclusive and magic-riddled world that the Dianello family inhabited. A world far removed from magic inspectors. So he decided to pay this old acquaintance a visit after work.

He didn't repeat his previous mistake to not have dinner or feed the magic sniffers and made sure that both were looked after before he left the house again.

Sabyna the witch lived a bit out of town, so he caught the train for a short ride to the foot of the mountains that formed the natural border between the harbour city of Tamba and the highlands where he had grown up and where people lived off the land and sold their produce to the city.

Further still was the border with the magical realms, but you had to get a special permit to travel there.

The train to his home town would take a few hours and the border was further still.

The trip was short and relaxing. The afternoon sun cast golden light over the coastline and the fields where cows grazed and crops grew.

Mothers and children with bags of shopping made up most of the other passengers in the carriage. The atmosphere was one of happy laughter. Perrin was reminded of about how he and Atreyo had been talking about taking in a young orphan to raise as a well-educated, happy citizen, but of course Atreyo's death had changed all that. Maybe it was time to revisit it again. After all, he now had a spare room.

The station at Jasmine Falls was only small, but most of the families got off here. Since the passenger train had started to run, many small-acre farmers had moved to this area for its fertile soils, while they could still sell their produce to the city of Tamba. With the farmers came their families and all the services that catered for families.

The woman Perrin was going to visit, however, had lived here for many years, long before the train stopped here.

Perrin was at a stage of his life where many of the people he dealt with every day were younger than him, but this woman was not one of those.

Sabyna was—there was no other way of putting it—a witch. She had come from the realms long ago as a young woman and had lived through the magical upheavals that resulted in Tamba's city council banning magic from its territory. She agreed with it. At least she said so.

But she was still a witch.

Getting to her house required Perrin to climb the hundreds of steps that started at the deep and dark pool at the bottom of the falls that gave the community its name.

The jasmine grew all over the mossy and slippery rocks and lined the steep staircase hewn into the cliff face.

The air was cool and humid, but Perrin was still hot and sweaty by the time he got to the little grassy park at the top.

During holidays, people with families would come here but today he had the park to himself. Those who made the effort to climb were rewarded with a magnificent view all the way over the city and to the offshore islands.

Sabyna's house lay tucked into the lush forest at the back of the park. Hers was the first in a small cluster of houses.

It had been a long time since Perrin had last been here, and it was a long time since he had seen Sabyna in town.

He pushed open the creaky gate and walked along the path of uneven flagstones through Sabyna's riot of a garden. At this time of the day, the smell of herbs and flowers hung in the air.

"Well, well, look who's here, Mr Fibbles. I didn't think I'd ever see him again," said a sharp voice from the front porch.

Sabyna sat on an old rocking chair basking in the last rays of sunlight. She was as thin as a whip, dressed in purple as usual. Her hair sat in a bun atop her head, although advancing age had thinned it a great deal. A number of gold and silver bangles hung from her ears, some adorned with ancient runes in tongues from the realms. She wore a lot of rings and arm bands and her precious emerald pendant lay, as usual, in the hollow atop her cleavage. Although the skin above was rather spotted and papery-looking these days.

Mr Fibbles, of course, was the ancient long-haired white cat on her lap. He had a green eye and a blue eye, but Sabyna had previously confessed to Perrin that the poor cat was rather blind.

"I haven't seen you in town for a while either," Perrin said, while stepping onto the veranda.

It struck him how he had just stepped into a time capsule, because while Sabyna looked older, the house, its riotous garden, the knickknacks on the veranda and the walls that always looked in need of a lick of paint, were still the same. The place smelled the same, too, of hearty soup mixed with an unidentifiable tang of something earthy and magical. Crushed leaves of aromatic herbs, peppermint oil, the sweetness of exotic, but poisonous fruits, the pungent odour of crushed stink bugs.

"Sit down, sit down." She gestured at a bench that stood against the wall. The bench was rather full of knickknacks, the largest of which was a metal-wire bird cage. "Just put the cage on the ground. The parrots will find it when they decide to return."

Perrin lifted the bird cage—with its door open—and set it next to the veranda steps. There was also another cage with a much more familiar animal. The fluffy brown creature reared up on its hind legs, poking its wriggly nose through the bars of the cage.

"You keep magic sniffers?" A very handsome male specimen, too. Well fed.

"Argh." She flapped her hand. "Some people are trying to trick me, don't they, Mr Fibbles?"

The cat had gone back to sleep.

"How did you get the Bureau to allow you to keep magic sniffers?"

"Argh. Those city people. They think they control what we do. If I want to buy a mountain rat, I buy a mountain rat. Nothing says I can't buy mountain rats, no?"

People who used the term mountain rat usually meant to say that they thought little of the Bureau's authority. They were the people who thought that magic should be officially allowed. Who apparently still wanted to know if someone tried to play a magic trick on them. Fancy that.

Perrin sat down.

She cocked her head while studying him. "But I hear you work for them now?"

Them. The Bureau.

"I do. But I didn't come here for that reason."

She snorted. He doubted she cared even if he had come here as an inspector.

"I'm sorry about Atreyo. It's a shock when someone dies when they're younger than me. What a waste, what a waste. They could have taken my old arse instead of a young man full of life."

"Sadly, that's life. You don't get to choose."

"That's right. That's life. Money's got very little to do with it. When your time's up, it's up."

"I have come for a reason, though." And he went on to explain his misgivings around the activity of Atreyo's brother and the screamer the family had received. While he spoke, Sabyna's face darkened and when he finished, she let a silence lapse.

"You want my advice?" And when he didn't say anything, she continued, "I guess you do, else you wouldn't be here."

"I want to know if you have any knowledge of what's going on. So I can help solve it. If you can shed any light on what he might have bought."

"Argh." She snorted. "This is my advice: do not get involved."

"But I already am, because I'm a magic inspector."

She lifted a finger. "Do not get involved. Just keep inspecting the inns and shops and that stuff that the inspectors do. This is bigger than all of the inspectors together and it's something that no one in Tamba is ready to handle."

"But they'll have to handle it, anyway?"

"Argh. It will be handled and it will pass, as all these things do, but anyone who's not involved shouldn't become involved, because then they won't be killed."

"That's what the Bureau is about: preventing people getting killed."

"Mark my words: ignore it. Let the wizards sort it out."

Well, wizardry wasn't allowed in Tamba, and there were no important wizards in town. So she was suggesting foreign wizards were going to come in and battle out some magical issue over the heads of the innocent citizens?

"Can you at least tell me what's going on?"

She heaved a sigh. "Well, I guess it all started with the death of the Grandwizard Fallon in Solania."

"I thought Grandwizards could live forever."

"No one can. Grandwizards—if they're smart and not all of

them are—can live longer than most people, but they must die. Fallon had lived a long time and had many fabled treasures in his collection. Many treasures that others wanted, or thought were theirs. Cursed treasures. Secret treasures, you name it and he had it."

"I understand some of those *were* actually the property of other realms."

"Aargh, yes. The Grandwizard wasn't always honest about getting the pieces he desired. After his death, the other Grandwizards bickered over who should get what, and a lot of stuff was distributed. But there was also a lot of stuff that was—shall we say—contentious. He got it in dubious deals and held objects hostage in return for favours or to avoid embarrassment. No one knew what all these arrangements were because he was good at remembering things and never wrote anything down. So after all the Grandwizards plundered his assets, there was a collection left over that no one would touch. It went from his family—who didn't want it and said it was cursed—to various authorities— who didn't want it either—to private collections. It was not that people didn't want the collection. Those collections are worth a lot of money."

Perrin knew. Atreyo would sometimes buy them.

"There was a lot of fighting between wizards about stuff that was in this collection. Many were pieces stolen from other realms. Some were so valuable you can't put a price on them. Others, from outside the realm, were after the stuff. Some people sent mercenaries to retrieve what they considered theirs."

"Pumans?"

She flicked her eyebrows. "If you know the story so well, why do you ask me?"

"It's nice to have one's thoughts confirmed. These are all guesses of mine."

"Ha. There is a reason Atreyo was interested in you. You're smart."

Huh, he'd never seen it that way. He thought Atreyo had been interested in him because he was quiet, dutiful and displayed little ambition.

"So tell me what happened to the collection."

"It went from hand to hand. Various bits were peeled off and returned to whomever claimed them. But also, a few people in possession of the main collection died mysteriously. And then the collection vanished."

"Let me guess, it turned up in Tamba."

She gave him a sharp look. "There have been rumours."

"No, I think I know where it is, or at least some of the items."

Another sharp look. "You do?" She no longer told him not to get involved.

"Well, I'm not sure, but I can make guesses. When Mirella visited me, I took the screamer the Dianello family had received to the Bureau and translated it for her. The family could have done that themselves, of course, but that would have meant admitting that they have illegal stuff, that they acquired illegally. And the Bureau has a public office, so they would have had their dealings exposed to public scrutiny. The screamer asked for the return of an item that belongs to Gaminia. Roban Dianello prefers to ignore the whole thing, perhaps judging that he's safe in Tamba."

"Ha! There is no such thing as safe."

"Exactly. Their office has been broken into, maybe by pumans hired by Gaminia. I'm guessing it started when Roban Dianello—not knowing what he was dealing with—saw the collection offered for sale and thought to make some quick money selling items to collectors like Atreyo used to do, but found it was more trouble than it was worth."

She shook her head. "The pursuit of money makes decent men do stupid and evil things."

"Men?"

"It's always the men. The heads of the family. Strutting around in their finery boasting about... stuff they bought. Trinkets. Rubbish. It's all about showing off what they have. Argh."

"There are rumours about a magical trumpet that's overgrown with barnacles."

She gave him a sharp look. "The Horn of Truth?"

"I have no idea. Apparently, members of his family have been trying to sell it, but no one is interested."

She whistled between her teeth. "People have been after that for a long time, since it was lost. If he truly has it..." She shook her head. "If he's indeed got it, he bought a big problem for himself. It's a Gaminian treasure, and Gaminia has employed many a bounty hunter to retrieve it. It's become somewhat of a legend even amongst pumans. There are rumours about fabulous bounties for returning it to Gaminia. I don't know what's true. I could believe that old Fallon squirrelled it away. I could even believe that he pulled off stealing it from the underwater palace, however he might have achieved that. Fallon was no friend of the whales, and the horn was their only way of talking to land creatures, although with Fallon, the art of using it will have died. If he has it, it's something only he can solve by returning it to Gamina. Because if Gaminia knows where it is, they won't stop at anything trying to get it."

"But if he's ignoring their pleas, it will only get worse."

"It will, until he takes action."

"The Bureau should put pressure on him. We should offer to help him."

"Don't, Perrin. Whales are very big and they can be very angry, and you can't argue with them, because they don't speak our language and don't think about life in the same way we do. We can't visit them and they can't visit us."

"But if the Bureau can't get involved, then why have a Bureau of Magic Abuse in the first place?"

"Don't you have some inns and eating houses to inspect?"

Perrin couldn't tell if she was joking.

CHAPTER 16

But if Perrin thought that he'd have the time to investigate quietly about what sort of items Roban Dianello might unwittingly have bought in this cursed collection, he was mistaken.

When he came into work the next morning—still tired from having returned late on the train the previous night—he found a man from the transport company waiting at his desk.

"You really need to take responsibility for this creature," the man said before Perrin had a chance to greet him.

Oh no, this was again about that infernal dragon.

"What has it done this time?" Perrin said while putting the magic sniffer cage on the desk and doing his best not to roll his eyes.

"That beast has almost destroyed the cage," the man said. "We've had a carpenter come in to put extra planks of wood to reinforce it. You'll be getting the bill."

Perrin opened his mouth—

"Yes, we gave it things it could destroy to keep it busy, as you suggested, but it won't be long before it breaks out and then you will have to pay for all the damage that it does to the warehouse. We are not a zoo. You really must put this creature somewhere else."

"I know," Perrin said, and he sighed. "I'm working on it."

But the truth was, he had run out of goodwill and out of places for the dragon. He had nothing, because he'd already burned through all the types of businesses that would normally provide this service.

So he assured, once again, that he would deal with the dragon soon. He could see in the man's face that he didn't have much trust that it would actually happen.

He then mulled over the very limited remaining options while doing his rounds through the inns with the magic sniffers.

Some people had even suggested killing the creature, and while he thought that was a repulsive thing to do, he also wondered if that was even possible.

Yes, Laeticia and her boyfriend Gaeron had raised dragons from eggs and killed them, but that was when the dragons were still very young and it was possible for a few people to subdue them.

The Bureau's mistake, of course, was to let the dragon grow as big as it had while trying to solve the problem diplomatically. When Perrin had finally obtained the funds to hire a truck to take the dragon back, the creature had been too strong for the truck. And the same happened with the train.

That left only one option. A boat.

Which the Bureau would never fund because they disliked anyone involved in shipping and sea trade.

But he could get Roban to pay for it... if he could get Roban to give him the item—the Horn of Truth—that Gaminia wanted.

He needed to be smart about this.

So, after he had finished his round of inspections and whizzed through his reports, he wrote down his plan. It was big.

He was not so crazy as to try to enact it without Inspector Carbin's knowledge, and when he went into the office later in the afternoon just before she was about to go home, he shut the door, because he envisaged there might be some shouting.

Several of his colleagues gave him suspicious looks as he went into the office. They knew he had been trying to find a solution for the dragon, and no doubt they had heard about his latest troubles.

Inspector Carbin read over his plan and didn't say anything for a while.

Then she looked up and met his eyes.

"It's courageous," she said. "A number of people could get very angry at you for trying this. If it fails. Especially if it fails. These are people we'd normally try not to anger. People who walk the moral high ground on dealing with pirates and such. Those who consider all seafarers pirates." Mainly those on the council.

"I understand and I agree. I would rather not have to do this, but I'm not sure what else we can do. We've tried everything, and it takes care of two problems at the same time. We absolutely need to get rid of that dragon. It's a danger to everyone in town."

She nodded. "Yeah." She blew out a breath. "Well, I wish you luck. This could cost us all our jobs, but I trust that you won't do things that are too silly. At least I'm glad it won't be me visiting the Dianello family."

Perrin left the office with a sense of deep dread in his stomach. He wasn't sure that the trust in him was well-placed.

He went back to his desk and spent some more time writing out a letter, and after he had checked and double-checked it several times, he copied it onto nice paper and took it to the house of the Dianello family.

Roban Dianello lived with his family in a house next

door to his parents. Perrin had never spent much time in this particular house, because the family always met at the parents' place, but since Roban was now the self-proclaimed owner of Atreyo's business, he should do this officially and professionally as a proper inspector of magic would.

He knocked on the door and when a servant opened it, said he wanted to speak with Roban about business. He was still wearing his inspector uniform, so he figured the man would suspect what this might be about.

It was all part of the game.

The servant asked Perrin to wait inside on a chair put next to the door for that purpose.

The house was not as old as the Dianello family home, and didn't carry the weight of history that made changing it almost immoral.

As a result, Roban had made changes to the house that made it more modern. Gone was the large and opulent hall that served only to impress visitors, but that sucked up heat and created a useless void inside the house.

The new hall—where Perrin waited—was functional and big enough for the things that people did in halls: store and put on their coats, wait for someone or receive deliveries.

The rest of the front of the house was a study and teaching space for Roban's teenage children and those children—a boy and twin girls—were completing some kind of science project when Perrin sat on that chair.

Voices drifted through the hallway, and Perrin thought he could hear the words *Magic Inspector*.

A moment later, Roban himself came to the hall.

He looked Perrin up and down, no doubt recognising him.

Perrin feared briefly that Mirella had talked about him, in which case he would see through the plan in less than a second.

And he would be angry, and accuse him of blackmailing, which he was trying to do—sort of.

As he stood here, he realised how he didn't know this man very well, because he always seemed a bit distant, and he'd found no special reason to dislike him, since Mirella and Atreyo's father already took up that space.

"Hmm, it's been a while since I've seen you," Roban said. "What brings you here?"

Perrin tried to find a denigrating tone in his words, but didn't hear it.

"I could spend a long time explaining, but it's best that I let this do the talking." Perrin gave him the letter.

Roban took it and unfolded it. Perrin watched his face while he was reading. He took quite a long time reading, and let an uncomfortable silence lapse after he had finished, but looked over the text again.

Perrin wondered whether he was going to get angry or tell him to go away. In which case, they might as well release the dragon because he had tried.

Then he said, his voice flat, "You want me to hire a boat to return a dragon to Solania? Why would I lend you a boat?"

"Because I need one and the Bureau doesn't own one."

He squinted at the letter. "But if the Bureau can't pay for its own boats, why should I have to?"

"Because I might reveal to the council that you have a thing called the Horn of Truth, which is the reason that we've been having trouble with pumans."

"Huh."

He looked at the letter again and then back at Perrin. Then he said again, "Huh. Come into the office and we'll talk further."

Perrin followed Roban through the hallway into a comfortable and widely spaced office.

Instead of the usual desk, and a chair to face the desk where the visitors could sit, this office consisted of a number of smaller tables with numerous chairs placed around them.

Not a regular office at all.

"I am not quite familiar with the type of business you do," Perrin said.

"We do a number of different types of business," Roban said, "but my wife and I mostly use this room to have meetings with our tutors."

"Tutors?"

"My wife runs a school where people can come to have private tuition."

"You mean children?"

"Yes, but also adults. We do all kinds of tuition. Whether it is for children or for adults. The other day we did training for fire-fighters."

It was interesting, and something Perrin filed away in the back of his mind.

He might not want to work with the well-off citizens of the town, but life became very hard if you took that position in public. They owned the businesses and had the money to make things happen, as he was experiencing right now.

Roban offered Perrin a drink, but he preferred to stay alert.

They sat down on a set of armchairs in the corner of the room.

Eventually, after making some small talk about how nice the furniture was, Roban began, "I wouldn't be amenable to making deals, but I admit I'm in a bit of a bind, and there might be something you could do for me in exchange for my cooperation."

It was indeed as Perrin had worked out.

"So it's true that you bought old Fallon's collection. Hoping to make a quick sale of the valuable items, and not knowing that the collection had already been picked over by magicians in Solania and only the troublesome items remained."

"If I find that swindler who sold it to me, I will have his head on a stake."

"You will have to come to the Bureau for that."

"I don't live under the illusion that you will be able to do more than I can do by myself."

"Maybe not, but at least it will have the endorsement of the council and the mayor, and that has to be worth something. As opposed to, for example, going to jail for serious misuse of magic."

Roban gave him a serious look and blew out a sigh.

Then he got to his feet.

"All right," he said. "I'll show you."

He preceded Perrin into a storeroom where he opened the door to an old cabinet. On the shelves inside stood boxes and jugs and jars, all crammed together and sometimes stacked on top of each other.

Vials of strange substances, contraptions with many arms and levers, ornate boxes, old books, bottles with potions and illegible labels, pots with dried herbs and much, much more.

Roban took a rusted metal case from the back of the top shelf. He placed it on a table in the room and opened the lid.

Inside the box, on a bed of dried seaweed, lay the fabled trumpet.

Just like the old man from the shop had told Perrin, it was encrusted with marine growths and didn't look like it would still produce a sound.

Perrin was not a magician, but as he set eyes upon the thing, his skin pricked. He swore he could feel the magic swirling around the room, coming from this ancient object of the sea.

He took in a breath, reached out to touch it, but withdrew his hand.

Roban said, "It's all right, it won't fall apart. It's quite sturdy despite the way it looks. It doesn't work, by the way. I mean—as a trumpet."

"Can't you feel the magic?"

Roban frowned.

"This is definitely the thing that Gaminia wants and that they've been turning over the city for."

"They can buy it back if they want."

"I don't think that's how it works. It was theirs to begin with. It was stolen from the palace in mysterious fashion."

"I bought the collection fairly."

"Many items in it were stolen or cursed. That was why you could buy it at a cheap price. Because no one else wanted it."

"That's untrue. I had to bat away other contestants for it."

"Locals from Tamba, no doubt, who had no idea what they were bidding on. Tamba was the only place where such a thing can be sold. Because everyone else would have known that the collection was trouble."

Roban said nothing. His mouth twitched. Then he blew out a breath. "Anyway, I want to be rid of this thing. It's endangering my family."

"That's why I have an offer."

"Ah. I could have known that you'd only become involved because you wanted something."

"That's often the case, and the same could be said about you. But in the end, you have a problem and I have problem, and maybe we can put the two together and come to an agreement."

Roban snorted. "Just tell me what you want and maybe we can talk business."

Perrin explained the situation he found himself in with regard to the dragon. The presence of the dragon in town was not exactly a secret, so he wasn't giving away key information here. As he spoke, he watched Roban's face grow increasingly dubious.

"So, to be short, you ask me to risk my business contacts with shipowners in order to transport this dragon back to the wizards of Solania who don't even want it back?"

"Don't tell me that you don't realise how much damage a dragon you can do in Tamba. And you're asking me to risk my life to go and return this thing to the whales?"

They looked at each other for a while, and Perrin could see the thoughts whirl behind his eyes.

After a while, Roban said, "Supposing I were to arrange a ship—and I stress to you this wouldn't be *my* ship because I don't own ships—could you take the whole collection back to Solania? I don't even care about the money anymore, I hate to think what other troublesome items are going to be in it. It was a mistake to buy it, and if I get my hands on the misfit who sold it to me, he will regret ever having met me, but meanwhile, I want to be rid of it."

Perrin grinned.

CHAPTER 17

Captain Anko stood on the deck of his ship with his arms crossed over his chest. He was a well-known figure in Tamba's shipping world, a towering man with broad shoulders and a head full of curly fox-coloured hair which he wore in a thick plait that hung over his shoulder and down the front of his leather vest.

His face held an incredulous smirk, as if he couldn't quite believe what he was hearing.

"You want me to do what?" he asked, and he laughed, a booming sound that echoed over the deck and adjacent quayside.

The ship next to Captain Anko's ship, the *Seven Winds*, was being loaded and the captain's loud laughter drew some curious looks from the dock workers lugging large sacks into the nearby warehouse.

"I know it is a strange job," Perrin said. "But you will be rewarded fairly for your efforts."

"Ho, but what is fair for a trip that is dangerous and might be a risk to my ship and my crew?"

"Roban Dianello stands as guarantor for the payment."

The man in question had said very little since he and Perrin had stepped onto the deck of the ship. He leaned against the railing, his arms crossed over his chest. He clearly didn't want to be there. Under normal circumstances, he would consider being forced into this arrangement as a sign of defeat.

Captain Anko snorted. "Ho, that's all very well, but neither of you landlubbers are going to carry the dragon on your ship."

Perrin said, "The dragon won't be your responsibility. The beast will be locked up for all of the journey. I will come with it, and we will provide all its food and look after its needs. The only thing you need to do is to make sure that we get to Solania."

"And stop off at Gaminia, right?"

"That should be easy. It's along the way."

"No, no, no, you don't understand. Nothing is easy about Gaminia. For any normal trip, we avoid the place like the plague. When you cross the border, it's like sailing into a floating net. A huge floating net. Every time you cut yourself loose, they come up with some other ridiculous permit they want you to have gotten."

"We will take care of that. I've already applied for the permits. We will be returning something that they have asked for. They will be happy to see us."

"Ho! That has to be the first time the whales are happy about anything to do with any creature that lives on the land. I don't like them at all. We normally sail along the coast to avoid them. It's a bit longer and there can be pirates, but I rather deal with that than having to decipher the nonsense spouted by these whales. There's stories of ships held up for weeks for some stupid thing, while the cargo rotted and then the whales accused the captain of fouling the water when they had to ditch the load."

Perrin was rather sick of the man's complaining. Since

coming on board, Captain Anko had only wanted to argue and make excuses.

"Look, we can stand here all day to talk about reasons not to go to Gaminia. I understand, I know, it's not an easy place. But Roban wants to have this troublesome item returned to the kingdom, and that is what you'll be paid for. The only thing you need to do is to provide transport and you'll be seen as a hero by all of Tamba. I will look after the rest."

The captain gave Perrin a sideways look. "Ho. I don't go much for this hero stuff. Most of those we call heroes are not half as great when you start looking closely. I'd rather be safe. And Roban wants me to do this?" He again looked sideways at Roban as if hoping that this was, after all, a joke of some kind.

Roban nodded and returned to his stare and his silence.

Perrin continued, "Roban obtained the trumpet by accident. We've worked out that the trumpet is the cause of the unrest and criminal activity in town. The reason why pumans have been roughing up people and breaking into businesses."

"And my crew."

"See? There is a benefit even to yourself."

"Hmph. As long as you do all the negotiation with those whales. They're nasty creatures. Not like the gentle giants that we are led to believe."

"Yes, we will deal with all of it," Perrin said.

"Well, I guess I don't have any reason to object. I still don't like it, mind, and you had better stick to your promises, and if something goes wrong, none of it is my fault, right?"

Perrin assured him that all he needed to do was to sail the boat. In fact, the further the captain and crew kept from the dragon or the trumpet, the better.

The captain reluctantly agreed to do the job. He still kept looking at Roban for signs that this was a joke or that Roban didn't really want this job done, but Roban had his own reasons to want this done. Perrin didn't even think he knew half of it, just that it put Roban in a difficult situation if found out. He didn't object, and Captain Anko had no reason to object either. A job was a job. Payment was good.

After the contracts were signed, Perrin went to the nearby animal warehouse where he instructed the people to make sure that the dragon's crate was solid and that it stood in a position where it could easily be moved.

While he was in the warehouse, the dragon snorted and stomped around in the cage, occasionally pressing its snout or backside against the bars on the tiny window. It blew hot breath into the warehouse. Warehouse workers jumped if they spotted the dragon's behind. In the time Perrin hadn't visited, the workers had hammered extra planks of wood against the lower end of the window, on the outside of the bars. To prevent further "accidents", Perrin guessed.

"When I remove the creature, you're going to have to pay for heating again," Perrin said, his attempt to make a joke.

The warehouse owner didn't think it was funny. "What's to say you won't be back here soon enough?"

"Let's hope not," Perrin said.

"No."

His voice was dead serious, and Perrin's cheerful mood fell flat.

He hoped he now had the problem solved. But what if this failed again? If the dragon destroyed the ship and the Bureau would have to pay Captain Anko. Imagine how furious the mayor would be then. Perrin could already hear the screeching *And I said that we should keep the beast here.* By the heavens, no. It didn't bear thinking about. If that happened, then he would really have to let the beast go.

He made doubly sure that the warehouse workers secured the crate.

What's to say you won't be back here soon enough?

No.

Definitely not.

If it failed, he would kill the dragon. However one killed dragons. He wasn't sure that was possible, and to be honest, he'd rather not find out.

It took him the entire length of the walk from the harbour to the Bureau to recover from these maudlin thoughts.

Something was happening. That was good, right?

Upstairs in the office, he asked to see Inspector Carbin.

She seemed quite surprised but led him into her office, where he shut the door. She sat down at her desk, which was overflowing with account books. Wonderful. She was going to be touchy about money.

"I need some time away from the Bureau to travel."

Her eyebrows flicked up.

"I've found a boat, and I've arranged for the dragon to be taken back to Solania via sea. I'm going to travel with it so that we can be sure it gets there and won't come back to bother us anymore."

"You did what?"

"I got a boat."

"How much is that going to cost?" Sure enough, there was the money.

"Nothing."

"Nothing ever costs nothing."

"Roban Dianello is paying for it. I've agreed to solve a problem of his in return."

She narrowed her eyes into small slits. "Why don't I like the sound of that?"

"Do you like that any more or less than the prospect of an animal park with a dragon, or, following the dragon's escape from the park, a dragon loose in the city? And oh, can the Bureau just catch this beast that's made a nest on top of the town hall and take it elsewhere? And yes, we know we make a great big deal over merchants bringing in magic buttons, but we just forget about the dragon? Take your pick."

She looked like she was going to argue, but then she let out a heavy breath. "Just…" She held up her hands. "Just don't tell me about it, so I can't be accused of being complicit in a crime."

"Don't worry. I have no intention of doing so."

"Good."

"I presume that means I can go?"

"Just get out of here."

Perrin turned around, but he had barely touched the door handle when she said, "Perrin?"

He turned around again. "Yes?"

"Do you need to go alone?"

Perrin shrugged. "I don't know. Do I need to?"

"That was not a question."

"Oh. You want me to take someone?"

"Well, if you want. If you… think that whatever you'll be doing will pass scrutiny once we report this to the council. I think… it's probably better that you don't go alone. For your safety."

"I guess…"

"Take your pick."

Perrin didn't have to think about that. "Verbena."

"You like the kid, right?"

"Yeah. She's a fighter."

"She's really young. There might be… rumours."

"There would also be rumours that I'm not that way inclined. Everyone else at the Bureau is young, too. There would be worse rumours if I took a young boy."

"True. Ask her."

"That means the Bureau will pay for it?"

Was that a cringe he saw? "I'm sorry, but I have to know. If she comes, I'll have to buy some things for her and I'll need an account for that."

She narrowed her eyes.

"Verbena lives with her sister and her sister's seven children from seven different men, not her husbands. She is—sorry about the crude language—a whore. Verbena is the family's only ticket out of poverty. If I'm taking Verbena, I'll have to buy the kids some supplies."

Her expression softened.

"Just do it. You're way too decent a man to work here. Buy your stuff. Don't tell me anything else."

"I won't."

"Also, make sure that your magic sniffers are well looked after," she said.

Of course.

Through the window in Inspector Carbin's office, Perrin had noticed that Verbena had come in. She sat at one of the desks at the back of the room, the cage with her magic sniffers on the ground.

He asked her to come into the hallway with him and told her what Inspector Carbin had just said.

Verbena's eyes widened. "Really? I can come with you to...."

"Gaminia and Solania. Mind you, we won't be seeing much of either country."

"But that is..." Her eyes were bright. And then her expression sobered. "But what about my sister?"

"We'll buy some food for her."

"But she won't know how to cook it, and the wood has run out for the month, anyway."

"It might do her good to understand how much you do for her. She might stop treating you like you need to solve all her problems and do all her work."

"But the kids..."

"How old are they?"

"Clover is twelve. The others are all younger."

"Could you tell her what to do?"

"I guess I could. She's quite good."

"See. They'll be fine. You'll be back. They'll survive. You'll have to move to a place of your own one day."

"I guess... I would really like to come."

"Then come. We'll make sure that they can look after themselves for a few days."

"But who will look after the magic sniffers?"

"Stop thinking up excuses not to come. Bring yours to my place. I will ask Dorella to feed them."

He would be away for a couple of days at the most, and he was already looking forward to coming back and resuming his quiet life. Without the dragon, or screamers, or Mirella.

CHAPTER 18

By the time Perrin went home, he still wasn't absolutely sure that Verbena would come.

"The ship leaves tomorrow morning. Captains are beholden to the wind and the tides, so if you want to come, better be on time."

"Am I ever not on time?"

That was a good point. She was very punctual, despite all the nonsense her family put her through.

"Verbena, just tell your sister that you're going. Don't ask her, because she'll say no."

"What if she starts yelling at me?"

"Then you pack your things and bring them to my place. I mean it. I understand that you need to help your sister, but there is helping and then there is being taken advantage of."

"You think she's taking advantage of me?"

"She is! You bring in money, you help look after her kids, and you tell her to get rid of bad boyfriends."

"Not that she listens…"

"See? That's her choice and her life. You should look after

your life. And that doesn't mean you can't help her, too. You are helping. We are helping. Just not for everything."

"Yeah." She still didn't look convinced.

"Be there. Because if you're not, the ship leaves without you. And I could use a pair of hands."

Perrin walked home. When he got there, he instructed Dorella on how to look after the magic sniffers. She had a lot of questions, such as what to do when animals looked unwell. Perrin said he would make sure an inspector visited to check the animals out.

Then he needed to pack.

What did one take on a sea voyage?

Sailors usually wore sturdy clothes. He had some of those.

Would he need to consider getting wet? He had read that one needed to stick the bell of the Horn of Truth in the water for it to work. Surely that would result in getting wet when sitting in a small dinghy on the surface of a choppy sea.

Perrin dug his bathing suit from the back of the wardrobe. It released a waft of stale air when he shook it out. A hideous thing it was, too: adorned with broad red and white stripes like those cushioned floaties that sailors threw overboard in port so that the ship didn't bang too hard into the quayside with rough weather. Like Verbena's socks.

Great.

Well, he hoped he wouldn't need that.

He also tossed in a thick jacket and sturdy boots, his notebook and pens and the case with the trumpet.

He spent most of the night tossing and turning and worrying.

The sun had not risen when he lugged his bags downstairs, said goodbye to Dorella, who was in the kitchen preparing for the day, and made his way to the harbour.

He was out in the street before he realised that he'd heard nothing from Verbena. Did that mean she wouldn't come?

The *Seven Winds* lay ready to sail. The loading gangplank had been pulled in, leaving just the one for the crew. A man from the harbourmaster's office stood on the deck talking to Captain Anko.

Behind them, in the space between the main mast and the crew cabins, stood a giant crate that hadn't been here yesterday.

A crate with a little window. Something large and scaly moved within.

"He's not very happy," said a young female voice.

Verbena. Thank the heavens. She leaned on the railing and was looking into the crate.

"I wouldn't stay there if I were you. The dragon will just turn around and squirt straight at you. Then you'll have to spend the entire journey in smelly clothes."

"Just as well I've brought a spare set," she said. But she moved away anyway.

"And by the way, the dragon is a she, not a he."

"No kidding! How do you know that?"

"Because of her behaviour."

The harbourmaster's clerk had left, and Captain Anko introduced Perrin and Verbena to his crew. There were only three: two deckhands, a sturdy young man, Quinn, and his sturdy, short-haired sister, Ivy. She looked as unlike as someone called Ivy should look, according to Perrin: dreamy, willowy, magical. There was nothing magical about Ivy. Through her short hair and all along her shoulders and exposed skin on her arms, she sported enough tattoos that someone might be forgiven for thinking that they were a magical part of her skin. They changed colour, too.

Her brother was much less flamboyant, but also quite a bit taller. He'd said nothing during the introductions.

There was also the first mate, a grey-haired man called Hix—although the captain said that wasn't his real name—who looked after the ropes and sails and did the cooking while they were at sea. Captain Anko himself did the navigation and offered to take Perrin and Verbena on a tour.

"Mind you, if you expect luxury, then you should have bought a place on a holiday ship." He laughed loudly at his own joke.

Hix said nothing and slunk off as soon as he could.

He looked like a really friendly character. He'd get on fabulously with the dragon. They could hold crankiness contests.

Captain Anko allocated Perrin and Verbena a cabin below the deck at the end of a narrow corridor. It was very cramped down here. Captain Anko was almost too tall to walk straight.

The cabin had a tiny porthole window which looked out low over the surface, and a bunk bed.

"You didn't say you'd be bringing a helper, so you got to share the cabin. You better have no problem with that, because there is no other space." His loud laughter was earsplitting in the confined space.

When Perrin and Verbena had both dumped their bags on the floor, the cabin was full. There was barely enough room to turn around.

A narrow door at the end of the belowdecks corridor led into the cargo hold.

The main avenue to load the goods was with pulleys through the hatches on the deck, but they were all closed—with this cargo having been loaded yesterday.

The dark space was full of boxes of goods.

The ship was carrying a load of dried fruit like raisins and figs and jams, also dried sausages and spices.

The air was heavy with the scent of a well-stocked grocery store.

Against the far end, in the pointy end of the space, stood a load of barrels that contained cider and wine for the Solanian well-off citizens.

Apart from the crate containing the dragon, two massive crates sat on the deck with the text Cassock Foundry on the side. There was a small hole in one of the planks. Perrin tried to peep inside, but it was too dark.

Captain Anko said behind him, "Those are our prized cargo: two new bells for the city tower of the Solanian Grandwizard's palace."

"Are those bells this big?"

"These are medium-sized. Last year we transported the town bells for Validor and we had to make two trips because only one of them would fit."

"They must have been pretty heavy."

"That's why we have the crane up here."

Also the reason this ship could take the dragon.

Perrin also spotted the crate of pumpkins to feed the dragon. Good. So he wouldn't need to ask about it.

That very dragon took a mild interest in the goings-on, having turned inside the crate so that its orange-flecked eye caught the light.

"Oh, it's looking at me," Verbena said.

"As long as that is all it's doing."

Verbena approached the crate, grabbing a pumpkin. The young deckhand Quinn watched her, his gaze never leaving her.

Verbena was oblivious to his stares.

"Here." She worked the pumpkin through the bars on the tiny window. The dragon stopped it falling to the ground with her nose. A loud crunch came from inside the crate. Oh, well, that was the pumpkin.

"See, it likes food. Just like a dog." She stuck her hand through the bars and patted the dragon's nose.

"A dragon is not a dog," Perrin said.

"No, but some of the dogs on the quay are dragons."

Perrin couldn't argue with that. Still, the most vicious wild dog had nothing on the dragon in terms of size.

"Just make sure you only feed it those pumpkins," he reminded Verbena. "Absolutely no meat."

"I know."

Departure would be a little while off yet, Captain Anko said, because he still needed to get the export permit for the sausages and the harbourmaster had not yet allocated the ship a slot to leave. The tide was too low for ships this size to comfortably sail out.

Perrin went down the narrow stairs to the cabin, where he hung both bags on hooks next to the door. It smelled stuffy down there, but the porthole didn't open. Probably because it would be under water a fair bit when out at sea.

When the kitchen bell rang, Perrin joined the rest of the crew in the dining room on the top deck.

This was next to the galley, where the ship's first mate Hix had procured tea and sweet bread.

The tea was very strong and aromatic, very much unlike Dorella's tea. The other crew put a lot of sugar into their cups, and Perrin was forced to do the same.

While he'd been down in the cabin, Verbena had struck up a conversation with Quinn and Ivy—but mostly Ivy, because Quinn didn't say much, not even when asked a question.

Captain Anko squeezed himself into the tiny space. Through the serving window into the galley, Hix cast angry looks into the dining space. With Perrin and Verbena added on board, there was barely enough room for everyone, so Hix would have to stand.

It didn't look like Hix wanted to come in, anyway. He banged about with pots and pans at the stove, while the crew talked chit-chat.

Verbena asked the young deckhands how long they had worked on board this ship. Quinn seemed too astonished to reply, but Ivy said, "Only two months, mind. We were living on the docks before. I know you from over there. People talk about you in the drinking holes and that. Not that I go in there much. Just to find jobs, you know? We were lucky that the Captain wanted us. Not me so much, but Quinn, because he's strong. And he doesn't chat and have questions. You tell him I want that load of bags in the hold, then he puts them there."

Quinn continued eating his sweet bread without giving any indication that he was aware that he was the subject of the conversation. He kept looking at Verbena, who sat next to him.

Perrin made a mental note to mention to Verbena to be careful around Quinn. He was strong, and in the past, Perrin had seen these types of transfixed obsessions by young men of few words end badly. The ship hadn't even left the harbour yet. They had a few days to get through safely.

"Excuse me, Captain Anko?" a female voice called outside the cabin.

A woman in a harbour patrol uniform came to the door.

"The permits are done. You're cleared to sail."

CHAPTER 19

The crew sprang into action immediately.

Captain Anko went with the woman, Hix abandoned the galley and Quin and Ivy finished the last of their tea.

Perrin faced Verbena across the table.

"I guess we're off then," he said.

"Exciting. I've never left Tamba."

"Not at all?"

She shook her head.

"Not even on the train to Jasmine Falls?"

"We don't have money for the train."

"You have money to go by yourself."

"Yes, but then I'd have to answer questions about what I was doing and why I had to spend money on a ticket while the kids need clothes or stuff like that."

Perrin was certain: Verbena needed to find a place for herself. If she wanted, he could help her.

"Come on, let's watch while we sail out."

There was a bench on the rear deck that stood with its back

against a store compartment for ropes, a spare anchor, buckets and scrubbing brooms.

During his past sea travels, Perrin had learned that this bench was called the landlubber's station, because in rough weather it was the spot where one was least likely to be seasick. But also, sitting there meant you were out of the way of the crew while they were busy.

Perrin and Verbena sat here while the ship sailed out of the harbour. Verbena pointed out all the unusual things she noticed while the cramped houses of Tamba's harbour district slid from view.

They sailed past the pier, where rock fishermen watched the ship sail out and waved at the crew, past the lighthouse where the lighthouse keeper was cleaning the windows of the tower, and then into the open sea.

The weather was mild, with sun peeping between white clouds against a bright blue sky, with a mild breeze that filled the sails, but that wasn't strong enough to create a strong swell.

When the crew finished hoisting the anchor, rolling up the ropes, pulling in the floaties that had indeed the same pattern as Perrin's swimsuit, and stowing all those things in their places, Perrin ventured away from the bench.

It was a funny thing, walking on a boat. It reminded him of his trips with Atreyo, when they would travel to look at collections and fine wool, gorgeous fabrics, gemstones and aromatic spices.

The deck moved but not too much and it was possible—only just—to walk across the deck without holding onto something.

Perrin made a somewhat drunk stumble across to the dragon's crate.

He couldn't see the dragon through the little window—it was too dark inside and he didn't want to get too close. But he could hear the dragon snorting and rummaging in the straw.

Verbena walked in a similarly drunk wobbly path to the crate with the pumpkins, heaved one out and carried it to the dragon's cage. It was too big to fit between the bars of the cage, so she used her Inspector's knife to cut it in half and dropped the halves in through the window.

Smelling a snack, the dragon caught the pumpkin halves before they hit the straw and bit into them with a crunch.

"No kidding. You feed it pumpkins?"

This was Ivy. She and her brother sat on the deck with the mound of fabric of a sail between them. Quin was checking the joints for split seams.

"That's how we keep everyone safe," Verbena said. "The dragon doesn't blow fire unless it eats meat, so we feed it pumpkins."

"Does it like pumpkins?" Quinn asked, in a rare occasion that he made his voice heard. In typical fashion, he fixed Verbena with an intense stare.

Verbena shrugged. "It's eating them. So I guess it does."

Something was up with this young man, Perrin was sure of that. He was going to do something unexpected, and he was not going to let Verbena take the brunt of it. He didn't think that, living in the harbour district with a sister like hers, she was as innocent as she seemed, but he wasn't willing to bet on it.

"Come, let's do some work."

Verbena laughed. "Work? What sort of work can we do here?"

"You thought transporting a dragon is without filling in forms and writing applications?"

"Haven't you done all of that already?"

"Yes, but if you want to be able to do this without my help later, then you have to know how to do it."

She snorted. "I guess..."

She shrugged and followed Perrin across the deck, down the steps and along the narrow hallway to their cabin.

Of course there was no real work to be done, but Perrin made sure that the door was shut behind them before he spoke.

"I want to warn you," he said in a low voice.

"For what?"

"That boy. He's up to something. I don't like the way he looks at you."

"Men look at me like that all the time."

"Maybe it's time that you start taking notice of it. I'd hate for something to happen to you."

"Don't worry. I know where to kick them."

Perrin didn't think this was such a flippant matter, but he also wasn't at all certain that young Quinn would intend to harm her. Not at all. Just that he seemed to be obsessively transfixed with Verbena and, in Perrin's experience, this could end badly.

So he gave Verbena one of Atreyo's magic books to look at, and they spent the rest of the afternoon talking about the strange and wonderful things she found.

Perrin lit the oil lamp when it got too dark in the cabin to see.

When the bell rang, they went to dinner, which was a quiet affair. Ivy seemed to have run out of questions, Hix was his usual cranky self, Captain Anko took his plate to his cabin because he was plotting their course.

Perrin had spotted a table full of maps when walking past the open door to the captain's cabin.

Ivy's brother Quinn wasn't at dinner. Perrin wondered what the boy was doing, and at the same time also didn't want to know.

After dinner, he sent Verbena back to the cabin and went up the deck to make sure that the dragon was happy and fed.

By now, only a faint glow of daylight remained on the horizon, and the sparse lights on the deck didn't allow him to look into the crate. But the smell of dragon poop was overwhelming. He'd have to shovel out the cage tomorrow. He didn't look forward to that job.

To get to the staircase that led to the cabin, he had to walk past the captain's cabin and the galley. A light glowed within the galley. Captain Anko and Hix sat at the table, with jugs of some drink—probably beer—between them.

Perrin said, "Goodnight," and continued around the corner to the entrance of the stairs.

But there he got a fright, because someone was sitting on the "landlubbers bench".

Quinn.

"Sorry, I didn't see you. It's so dark here." He noted a glint of light just behind the boat, and a wicker basket next to the bench, with inside a roll of gut string. "Are you fishing?"

"Yes, but also I'm keeping watch."

"What are you watching out for?"

"Pirates. Have to warn the captain if there's any coming."

"Are pirates common?"

"We see them sometimes, but the captain says we have a ship coming up behind."

"What? Out there?" Perrin peered into the ink darkness of the sea. Tiny white foam heads on the occasional wave faded into the night. He couldn't even see the horizon. "How does he know?"

"There is nothing on the seas that Captain Anko doesn't know."

By some means of magic, Perrin guessed, but since they were now officially no longer in Tamba, he couldn't complain about that.

"Are these... pirates something we need to worry about?"

"The Captain says we're gaining on them, and also once we

cross into Gaminia, they'll turn around. The whales hate pirates."

"Are those kinds of pirates dangerous? Are they following us specifically or are they just on the same course?"

"Who knows? But most pirates are cowards. They rather run than fight. They try to sneak up at night. That's why I'm here."

"Thank goodness for you, then."

CHAPTER 20

Perrin didn't think there was anything in that conversation to worry him. He was glad that Quinn didn't ask anything about Verbena. Maybe his worry was not warranted.

If he had to be perfectly honest, he thought Quinn was a bit simple. That could be why he stared at people, not just Verbena. He might even have some giant blood.

There was not much to do in the tiny cabin, so they went to bed early.

For the fact that he hadn't been away from home for close to a year now, Perrin slept very well, even if the bedding smelled musty and the bunk was quite narrow.

He woke up because of some heavy stomping above his head.

Urgh. Where was he?

Faint light filtered through the porthole window from the pre-dawn.

There was a pale oval that was Verbena's face in the space between the bunk above him and the ceiling.

"Are you awake?" she asked.

"I am now."

"What's that noise?"

"I don't know."

The noise was little more than a memory, heard in a state of semi-sleep when his brain had still been trying to figure out if this was a dream.

But then it came again: a scratch and a thump, followed by a shout from a male voice.

Perrin jolted upright, almost hitting his head on the bottom of Verbena's bunk.

"The dragon!"

He jumped out of bed without thinking about whether it was appropriate for Verbena to see his hairy legs, yanked on his trousers and shirt.

Verbena grabbed the clothes she had hung over a hook on the wall next to the top bunk.

Perrin pulled on his socks and stuffed his feet into his shoes, while Verbena slid from the top bunk.

A couple of thumps on the upper deck made the wooden structure shake.

"Bring the thunderstaff," he said to Verbena.

"I thought you said it didn't work anymore?"

"It's better than nothing."

He half-ran, half-stumbled up the steps, because overnight the sea had become rougher and it was now harder to walk in a straight line. Verbena was right behind him.

As they reached the top of the stairs, Captain Anko yelled, "Begone with you, evil beast!"

Perrin raced around the corner of the cabins.

And the sight that greeted him there filled him with horror.

There was a dragon on the deck of the ship. And it wasn't their dragon.

A beautiful, shiny, red-scaled creature with fully-formed

frills around its head and along its neck. It was huge. Curls of smoke trailed from its nostrils. It was a *male* dragon, judging by the pink protuberance dangling from the bottom of its abdomen.

As far as Perrin could see, his dragon was still in the cage. She was moving around in there. An eye with bright orange flecks moved behind the bars.

She was a female dragon and had shown nesting behaviour. Of course, she had noticed, heard or smelled the male, and now she was making soft little noises. Crooning, turning him on.

Captain Anko, Hix and Ivy stood in between the crate and the male dragon. The three crew members held a wholly inadequate shortsword, a broom, a piece of wood for a shield, and a long stick between them. The sword was Captain Anko's, and he brandished it in a vaguely threatening manner that betrayed he was no sword fighter.

The dragon calmly regarded the human crew, as if languidly deciding whether to eat them raw or burn them first. It was really the most magnificent animal, with the skin deep red and his eye moss green.

"Where did he come from?" Perrin asked.

"It came out of nowhere," Ivy said.

Verbena came onto the deck next to him, holding the thunderstaff aloft.

"I think he must have smelled our dragon," Perrin said. He gestured at Verbena. "Come on, let's scare him off. Give that to me, I have a lot more experience with that thing."

He took the thunderstaff from her.

Its metal surface felt familiar under his hands. When the dragon had first come into the Bureau's possession, he'd used it quite a bit.

He aimed the point at the male dragon. The head was the most effective place to target. He pressed the top and bottom buttons at the same time—and a spray of magic shot forth, much bigger than it had been in Tamba. It hit the dragon in the head. It let out a roar and stumbled backwards. Then it shook itself and jumped over the railing of the ship, wings outstretched. It skimmed the water and then rose slowly.

Captain Anko came to stand next to Perrin, still panting from the fight.

"How did you do that?" he asked.

"Thunderstaff," Perrin said. "Mind you, it mostly frightens the beasts. They get used to it and then it doesn't scare them anymore."

"Hopefully it won't come back."

Perrin wasn't so sure. He wanted to be in Solania already, so that the big dragon could be someone else's problem. His dragon in the crate was rubbing herself against the wooden sides. A scorch mark surrounded the window, and a crack ran along the side. She was still making that funny noise. About to spew fire? Or to attack and eat them all? She shouldn't be able to spew fire, but yet, all the signs were that she could. And that broken crate would not hold her in much longer. It was a wonder that she was still in the crate. Cowering from the much bigger male? Had she tried to defend herself from him?

But no, wait, the soft noise was coming from another part of the deck. From a pile of crab pots, to be precise.

Quinn sat there, with a crab pot over his head, whimpering.

"What are you doing?" Perrin asked.

Quinn lifted the contraption off his head. "Is it gone?"

"Yes. No thanks to you—wait, what is that?"

Quinn was holding a fish in his hand. "This?" He held it up. "I caught it." His eyes were wide. "I can fish on the deck, can't I?"

"Yes, but you weren't feeding the dragon fish, weren't you?"

"Me?" His face turned red.

"By the seven hells, what did I tell you about the dragon? Don't feed it meat!"

"But… pumpkins! How can a dragon be happy eating pumpkins?"

"I don't care if the dragon is happy or not, you do *not* feed it meat when I say not to feed it meat."

As Quinn cowered and pushed himself further into the pile of crab pots, a cracking noise came from behind Perrin.

The dragon pushed her front paws against the side of the crate. It split open, and the crack grew and grew. First came a clawed paw, and then a leg, and then a snout with a wide open nostril. The dragon used its head to push at the opening. Wood cracked. The Bureau's dragon-safe crate—supposedly indestructible—fell in pieces to the deck.

The dragon stepped out and stood on the deck underneath the sail. She shook herself like a dog. She was still wearing the metal collar and the chain, which was attached to the heavy base of the crate.

She jumped forward. The chain yanked taut, and she dragged the base of the crate along the deck. It was very heavy and only moved a bit, but enough for the dragon to be a menace to most of the deck.

"Defend the ship!" Captain Anko shouted, waving his sword. "You, too, useless lump!" The latter directed at Quinn.

Hix brandished his stick while protecting himself with the sheet of wood. Ivy bravely held the broom.

Quinn crab-walked backwards away from the dragon, picking up a rake along the way.

"Drive the beast back into the cage!" Captain Anko yelled.

The dragon did not show any signs that she wanted to attack, but if these idiots kept going like that, this would change in a heartbeat.

"Stop," Perrin yelled.

Captain Anko turned to him, his face red with anger. "You said that this crate was adequate to hold this creature. Use your magic wand to put it back in the cage. We'll fix the crate up. I have some very heavy tower bells to hold it in place."

"The staff won't work," Perrin said. "This dragon is used to it."

"Then what are we supposed to do? How do we get it back into the cage?"

"Into that broken cage?"

"You have to contain it. The dragon was your job, you said. It's my job to sail the ship and I can't do that if I can't reach half the deck of my ship."

"Which parts do you need?"

"How about: all of them?"

"Which are the most essential? The sails, the anchor, what else? Most of the other stuff is cargo, right?"

"We need to be able to get into the mast."

Perrin looked around desperately. Maybe they could use a fishing net, but he didn't see any handy nets or any ropes that looked strong enough to keep the dragon still for more than a few seconds.

They stood looking at each other for a while. The crew with their makeshift weapons. The dragon under the mast, looking back. Hix was frowning at the crane for loading the cargo overhead. It was attached to the top of the cabin. It should be possible to climb from the crane into the mast. The dragon was still chained to the heavy base of the crate. It wouldn't be able to climb.

He studied all the ways one could still get around without crossing the dragon's path.

Meanwhile, the dragon was not doing any of its usual things. Not hissing fire, not lashing out at the crew. Not even—heaven forbid—trying to drench them in piss.

The animal's behaviour was odd. She looked... stressed, for all Perrin knew. She swayed her rear end from side to side. She nosed around on the deck. She found a couple of hessian sacks, nets and sail cloth and pushed them into a heap.

"All right, this is what we're going to do," he said in a low voice. "We'll push the remains of the crate over to close off the side deck on both sides of the cabin. Then there won't be any way for the dragon to get to us."

Captain Anko's eyes widened. He understood.

If the deck was blocked, at least the crew could go below deck and to the captain's cabin.

Perrin helped Hix to distract the dragon while Verbena and the young deck hands shifted the heavy panels of the broken crate. They just fit in between the railing and the cabin, and a few extra boxes completed the job.

The dragon simply watched while they were doing this. It hissed a few times when they were getting too close.

A few uneaten pumpkins lay in the straw that had been in the bottom of the crate, as well as a spit ball consisting mainly of pumpkin skins. And a fish head. Ew and yes, he'd been right about Quinn feeding the dragon fish.

It also explained the dragon's lack of interest in food. Dragons were like birds and didn't eat when a spit ball was about to come up.

The dragon nosed around in the heap of nets it had collected. Then it turned around, lifted its tail and crouched on the sails.

"Hey, don't poop on my spare sails!" Captain Anko yelled.

But the dragon produced something creamy white, rubbery, about the size of a cabbage, that lay glistening in the nest of nets. It produced another one, and another one.

"It's laying eggs," Captain Anko said.

Yes, it was.

But Perrin was sure that male dragon had not made its way into the cage, even if it had tried very hard.

Maybe dragons laid eggs like chickens. They would just... start laying eggs when reaching maturity, male dragon or no.

And so much about the dragon's behaviour was starting to make sense. The increasingly irritated aggression—that was the instinct to stake out a spot for the nest. The pissing out of the cage—marking its lair. And on top of that, humans poked and prodded her, loaded her onto scary, noisy and smelly vehicles while feeding her a vegetarian diet. Meanwhile, she could feel changes in her body that caused discomfort. The eggs were still coming. In between each, she looked at the humans and the sky with alert eyes. Waiting for the male to come back? It would be too late now. Maybe for the next batch.

Oh boy, Perrin wanted to get to Solania before that happened.

Eventually, the eggs stopped coming. She nosed the sailcloth over them and then curled around them and went to sleep.

CHAPTER 21

The crew retreated to the galley, where they sat crammed into the narrow benches facing each other across the table, clutching mugs of strong tea.

A deep silence hung between them.

"It wasn't my fault!" Quinn blurted out after a long silence.

The rest of the crew clearly thought that it was.

"He told you not to feed the beast meat," Captain Anko said.

Quinn looked down.

"Please, I don't know whether feeding meat or not would have made all that much difference. The dragon is maturing. That is the cause of all this trouble."

"And you knew that?" Captain Anko said.

"No."

It was only partially a lie. Of course, he'd know that the dragon was growing, but just how close she was... no, he hadn't known that.

"What about I don't believe you," Captain Anko said, his arms crossed over his chest. "What about I just toss this dragon and you overboard?"

"Then you would have to deal with me," Verbena said.

Captain Anko laughed his loud annoying laugh. "You? A girl?"

"Yes. But I have many cousins and my sister has many loyal customers in the harbour district. Almost all of them work for the warehouses. I only have to say one word, and you'll have no one to load or unload your ships."

Captain Anko looked from Verbena to Perrin and shrugged. "Keep your hair on. I was only joking."

That didn't sound like joking to Perrin.

"Look, I will handle the dragon," he said, but as yet, he had no idea how.

The dragon was free, had probably been strong enough to break out of the crate for weeks, if not months. The only reason it didn't fly off was probably because of the eggs. Even if they were most likely blanks.

Perrin had no idea how they were going to handle a loose dragon when they got to Solania, but that was a bridge to be crossed when they got there. Solania had magicians who were undoubtedly better at handling dragons than anyone he could rustle up in Tamba.

The crew strengthened the barricade that stopped the dragon from coming to other parts of the ship and, for the rest of the day, Perrin remained on guard. Every time someone came near—for example Hix had to climb onto the roof of the captain's cabin and shuffle along a narrow beam to climb to the crow's nest—the dragon would rear up on her hind legs and hiss and flap her wings at the intruders.

Hix used some interesting and colourful language when he returned from the crow's nest, having run the gauntlet of fire spouts and flapping wings twice.

Perrin spent much of the rest of the day frantically going through his books to see if he could unearth any information about how to coerce a dragon into doing what you wanted. They were far too few to restrain it, and anyway, the large crate was thoroughly ruined. He was pretty sure that the dragon was not a type of creature that you could walk on a leash, and he would have to communicate with the port master of Solania to get a wizard to come on board the ship to deal with the creature. No doubt that would also cost extra, but he would just have to deal with that.

Perrin discovered a fair number of interesting things in the book. He'd skimmed through it many times, but never properly read the sections about magical creatures that were not living in Tamba, which was basically all of them. About dragons, it said that they were fiercely protective of things they considered theirs, as they had seen with the eggs, and that they were consistently more intelligent than anyone would think, although Perrin had not yet seen any evidence of that. But that had to be because the dragon was only young, and also because no one he knew was familiar with dealing with dragons.

After a quick meal shared with the others in an awkward atmosphere with very long and awkward silences, punctuated with silly questions, like *are we in Gaminia yet?* he retired to his cabin to read some more. He gave Verbena a book to help him. She asked some questions about magical herbs, but then said she was tired and went to sleep.

This time, he found it hard to sleep. Why hadn't he noticed previously how noisy this boat was? Several times he thought that something bumped the boat, but when he listened and held his breath, nothing further happened so he continued to pretend to lie in his bunk staring into the darkness at the bottom of Verbena's bunk.

But he must have fallen asleep because he woke up with a shock to a jolt that was definitely a bump from something hitting the boat from the outside.

"What was that?" he asked, but Verbena was already gone from the cabin.

He jumped out of bed, quickly got dressed, and ran up the stairs. He found the dining room empty, and all the crew on deck, leaning over the railing while hitting the surface of the water with sticks, and the dragon standing on the other side of the barrier, hissing and spewing flames at the water.

"The whales are attacking us!" Captain Anko yelled.

"Have we crossed into Gaminia yet?" Perrin asked.

Last night, Captain Anko had said this wouldn't happen until mid-morning, although how one determined borders within an ocean was a good question.

The captain had said there were supposed to be islands at the border. Perrin saw none.

But there were whales, at least three of them.

One swam alongside the ship. A huge head with a relatively small eye skimmed the surface of the water. Although the eye was still bigger than Perrin's hand. It moved and fixed on him before the whale disappeared back under the water again.

A second whale swam ahead of the boat. Its tail would come out of the water and slap on the surface. The third whale was behind the first one, watching from a distance. This one would stick a complete head out of the water and jump halfway out.

Then the one closest to the boat lifted its tail up and—whoa, it was huge—slapped it on the water. The sound was deafening. The resulting spray of water washed over the deck. Perrin managed to avoid getting his feet wet. The dragon spurted a gout of fire at the water, but all that was visible of the whale was a trail of bubbles.

"Why are they acting like this?" Captain Anko asked.

"I don't know. I'm not a sailor," Perrin called back from behind the crate.

"This is not normal behaviour. If the whales don't want us to come, they block the channel. They've never done this before. We always get permission to cross. This is because of you."

Many times? And here was Anko saying that they tended to avoid Gaminia.

But there was no time to argue.

A huge whale reared out of the water, head first. It rose and rose until it looked like it was going to jump right out of the water, and then listed sideways.

Perrin could see the tiny eye moving in the side of its head. The smell of ocean enveloped the boat, which looked tiny compared to the size of this creature.

The whale fell and fell, very close to the boat.

Splash!

Water churned and frothed. The whale's head hit the water with an almighty slap. A bigger wave crashed over the deck, drenching Perrin's shoes, the boxes and crates standing under the mast, and also the dragon's nest. She hissed as the water pulled at the bundle of nets and sailcloth, and stood on the cloth to prevent the nest from washing over the side with the foamy water.

The whale then lifted its tail and slapped it on the surface close to the hull. It could so very easily hit the deck and smash the boat to pieces.

"Do you hear that?" Hix yelled.

Yes, Perrin heard it: over the splashing of waves came a keening sound, rising from the water.

"It's the whale song," Captain Anko said.

"What does it mean?"

No one knew.

But Perrin remembered that he had something for that.

He ran back down to his cabin. He took his bag off the hook next to the door and retrieved the solid wooden box. Inside lay the precious trumpet that he had come here to return to the whales. Surely they'd recognise the sound, and they'd come to take delivery of it?

He lifted it out of the bed of velvet.

It was indeed a very rusty, barnacle-encrusted thing. If he hadn't known that this instrument had so much value, he would have discarded it. In fact, there might have been a real risk that Mirella might have done that.

He went back up the stairs with the trumpet.

Captain Anko gave him a strange look.

Now, how to use it?

He was too far from the surface to stick the instrument under the water, so he asked Quinn to hold his feet while he leaned as much as possible over the side.

It was very tricky, because the sea was rough and kept slamming him into the hull of the ship, and the whales were not helping by getting uncomfortably close. At one point, Perrin had to duck to avoid being hit by a giant front fin.

Perrin was afraid that he would be squashed between the huge body and the side of the ship. The spray from the waves hit him in the face.

When he stuck the trumpet in the water, a huge burst of noise came out of the mouth piece. It was so loud that even Ivy watching on the deck to help haul him back up clapped her hands over her ears.

"Can you hear what they are saying?" he yelled.

"You need to put it deeper in the water so that it stays submerged," Hix yelled.

So Quinn and Ivy lowered him further, hanging over the side of the boat by his feet. Thank goodness for quality shoes.

The waves washed over Perrin, and once he could even feel the tail of a whale brush his arm.

It was rough and made scratches on his skin that started bleeding. The seawater burned like fire.

He got thoroughly wet.

He put the trumpet in the water. It blurted out incoherent words *evil*, and *trespassing*.

He stuck the bell in the water again and yelled through the algae encrusted mouthpiece, "We have permission from the whale kingdom to travel through. I'm returning the Horn of Truth to you."

The response to his comment was a lot of incoherent screeching. He supposed this was a way to show their anger? He wasn't sure.

But whenever he stuck the trumpet in the water, he only heard garbled words.

And the whales would not let the ship through. They had arrived at the place where a passage between two islands provided access to Gaminia. Each time the boat moved forward, the whales formed a solid wall of bodies. They slapped their tails on the water. Those tails were really very big and strong. When the boat was too close, water would gush over the sides. The whales would have no trouble at all destroying the ship.

And since Hix had to loosen the sails, the boat was drifting with the current, straight for a rocky reef.

Captain Anko yelled, "Tighten the sails, we're turning back."

"I have to deliver the trumpet!"

"I don't care, I have to keep the boat safe. They're not letting us through. They know you have the damn trumpet. They can come and get it and ask for it politely."

Perrin couldn't argue with that. Those islands looked barren and uninviting, and that's where they'd be stuck if the whales destroyed the ship.

Quinn pulled him up. He was thoroughly wet and cold. This was not at all as easy as he had thought.

CHAPTER 22

The boat retreated and put out anchor in a bay of one of the islands, where they were out of the influence of the waves, but still very much within the line of sight of the whales that blocked the passage between the islands.

No one mentioned the option of going around the islands, so Perrin guessed that was not a done thing, for whatever reason—and to be honest, he could think of a few. They were, after all, in a land where magic could be used legally.

The island's shore looked as inhospitable close up as it had from a distance. The island was nothing more than a rocky knoll in the middle of the ocean, the home of a colony of seagulls and other birds that had turned part of the rocky shore white with their excrement. You could smell it, too.

The crew met in the galley, which was rather cramped when everyone was in there, and felt too small to hold this many people, especially when some of them were angry.

Captain Anko had, he said in a rant directed at Perrin and the dragon—which was stomping around on the deck—never been refused passage over Gaminia. That was a point of pride in his seafaring life. Landlubbers wouldn't understand what it was like being a sailor, navigating the different rules instated by the realms.

"Each of them just care about their own interests. Solania, Tamba, Validor, Gaminia, they're all just places we travel through on the way to another goal. It's our pride to get passage into all of them as easily as possible. We need to be able to go to all the realms. That's what my reputation is built on."

At this point, Perrin got rather irritated. He pushed himself up from the table. "Look, it's no good complaining. None of us knew that the whales would refuse us passage, even if we got the permits. The whales are known for pulling those sorts of tricks."

Hix said, "There is always a reason. The reason is that you are on board."

"We're coming to return something they want. Something they have sent thugs into Tamba to retrieve. Something that they are happy to run the risk of punishment for breaking into my brother-in-law's house!"

"Too right. It's to do with you."

"Stop arguing," Captain Anko said. "He's right about one thing: complaining gets us nowhere."

"That's why I will try again to talk with these cantankerous whales," Perrin said. "We're here because of them, and if they won't listen to us and accept that we're here to return the Horn of Truth, then we'll continue to Solania."

"We'll have to backtrack and it will cost the Bureau extra," Captain Anko said.

Of course! Perrin had to make an effort not to roll his eyes. "Let's just deal with that if it comes to pass. I don't particularly like it that thugs are making our city unsafe over this thing the whales want returned, so I will keep trying to give it back to them. Lend me a dinghy and someone to row it to the deeper water where the whales are."

Captain Anko agreed that Quinn could come. He was a strong rower, he said.

Perrin could believe it.

The captain also had a viewing tube, a metal cylinder the width of a bucket that was about waist-high and that was open on one side and had a glass window on the other.

Fishermen would use this device to look for oysters and clams, he said.

But all that would have to wait until the next morning. If the weather was good. And if the pirates that were supposedly still following hadn't caught up.

Back in their cabin, Verbena asked what she should do.

"Keep that dragon where it is," Perrin said. "I'll give you the thunderstaff."

"I thought it didn't work?"

"It doesn't. But it's the best we have."

"I was reading about dragons, and apparently some people train them like dogs."

"Those people are skilled magicians who work with an individual dragon as soon as it hatches."

"Isn't that what we've done?"

He met Verbena's eyes. She had a point there.

And what had Tamba done? Locked the dragon up because it was a *dangerous creature*. But, now that he thought about it, every act of aggression from the dragon could be explained by its fear of people and further mistreatment. Raised to be eaten. Tied up. Locked up in a crate. Fed a diet of only pumpkins.

He shrugged. There was little they could do about that now. "Just make sure it stays on the deck."

"What if the male returns?"

Perrin shrugged. "Try to chase it off, but if not, we might be forced to witness some dragon hanky-panky."

Verbena laughed. "You're so funny. Is that what you call it?"

"Well... you know what I mean, so it was an effective term. What would you call it, then?"

Her cheeks went red. "For dragons, I don't know."

Perrin was unaware that this activity needed a different word for different kinds of animals, but he was happy to let the subject rest.

THE NEXT MORNING dawned bright and sunny. There was little wind, and the pirate ship was nowhere to be seen. All those things meant that the trip was on.

Quinn and Hix lowered the dinghy from the back of the ship with a mechanism of ropes and a winch. Perrin then had to climb down a wobbly rope ladder to get into it. He got one of his arms wet because a wave sloshed against the side of the boat just as he was holding it off so it wouldn't clunk into the main hull.

For all his enormous size, Quinn was much more nimble.

Out on the sea, within a few strokes away from the ship, Perrin became aware of just how small and vulnerable they were, like a nutshell floating on the waves. The wind could easily smash them into the rocks. A whale only needed to bump the dinghy accidentally, flip it over, and they'd be in the water. Perrin considered himself a decent swimmer, but there were not many safe places here where he could swim to.

He busied himself cleaning the window on the viewing tube and then sticking it in the water so that he could see.

The window was very small and showed only a tiny sliver of water. The channel was quite clear but so deep that he still couldn't see anything, only dark green murk.

"Can you spot any whales?" he asked.

"Over there. Wait." Quinn grabbed the oars.

Not far from the boat, a fin stuck out of the water.

Perrin hovered in between telling him to get closer and back away. Boy, those whales were huge.

The fin disappeared, but now the animal's back came out of the water, blowing a spray of water out of the breathing hole.

"Right, I'm going to try this thing again," Perrin said. "Hold this." He nodded at the tube.

Perrin rummaged for the trumpet.

Quinn lowered the tube into the water and looked through the top. "I can see a whale!"

"That can't be the same one." Perrin looked as well. He didn't need the viewing tube. The whales were so close that he could easily see a much smaller whale and another big one. He also saw the animal's eye: tiny and roving. "I think they're looking at us."

He knelt awkwardly on the hard bench in the dinghy, stuck the trumpet in the water and blew.

A lot of bubbles came out, and a garbled sound.

Perrin put his mouth on the mouthpiece and yelled, "We ask permission to pass through. We have permits, obtained in Tamba. We are here to return a precious item to the king."

He waited, while holding the bell of the trumpet in the water. As before, this was not easy to do. The weather might be calm, but the dinghy still bobbed around a lot.

Were the whales going to respond?

If they wanted their trumpet, they had better.

The keening sound of whale song rose from the water. Some sputtering sounds came from the mouthpiece.

Then a clear voice said, "We gave you permission and no one else."

Just him? How did they think he was going to get through without a boat? "I needed a boat. Captain Anko says he's sailed through here many times."

Then the voice added. "Just you, humans. Not the creature. The evil one."

They were talking about the dragon.

"I'm taking it home to Solania so that it won't bother any of us again."

"You cannot take it through our lands."

"Then I also won't be able to return the Horn of Truth."

"What are you talking about?"

A wave washed the dinghy aside, lifting the trumpet out of the water. Perrin had to reposition the viewing tube. First, he only saw the whale's barnacle-encrusted side. This was so annoying and tiring. There had to be a better way.

"The Horn of Truth," he yelled through the mouthpiece. "The thing I'm using to speak to you now."

"You're a liar."

"I'm speaking the truth. Someone in my family accidentally bought a collection of items that he wanted to sell on the market. The Horn of Truth was in that collection. He truly didn't know that it belonged to you. I'm here to return it."

"You're still lying. You're taken in by their stories of nonsense."

"Whose stories? Aren't you glad I'm bringing it back, regardless of the stories?"

"Perrin." A hand tapped his backside.

Perrin had been so transfixed on what happened under the water that he hadn't paid much attention to what was happening on the surface. He raised himself from the viewing tube while the moving eye of the whale still observed him.

"Look."

Quinn pointed.

Another ship had turned up at the passage. Not a vessel from Tamba, but flying a flag with blue and white that Perrin didn't immediately recognise.

But he did recognise the chunky shape of the vessel. There had been a ship like this in the harbour on one of the days that Perrin was there looking for a temporary home for the dragon.

And that brought him to the most logical explanation.

"Pumans," he said.

Captain Anko had said that they were being followed by "pirates". But they were not random pirates. They were here for the trumpet. They were here for him.

Quinn said, "I don't know if they're pumans. The people on the deck all look normal."

"Pumans would not lower themselves to doing real work. They'll be in the cabin while the crew does the work."

"Should we go back?"

Perrin studied the strange ship. It was still coming straight for Captain Anko's boat, like they wanted trouble.

"Probably."

Quinn was big and beefy and would be of use if it came to a fight.

Perrin hoped not. He wasn't cut out for fighting, and it would be infuriating to lose the trumpet so close to returning it to Gaminia.

He packed the offending item in its box while Quinn took the oars.

Quite quickly, but still too slow, the dinghy made its way back.

But the new ship stopped short of the *Seven Seas*. From their position, behind the ship and low on the water, Perrin couldn't see what was happening to that ship.

Captain Anko stood on the deck, as well as Ivy and Hix. Verbena stood on the roof of the cabin from where she could see both the crew and the dragon, and could also look onto the other side where Perrin and Quinn were coming back.

She waved at Perrin and shouted, but her words were blown away.

"Are they pumans?" Perrin shouted back, but he didn't think Verbena could understand him, either.

They arrived at the *Seven Seas* and clambered up the ladder and then looked out to the other side.

The scene was one of utter chaos.

The whales surrounded the other ship, hitting their tails on the water and jumping out, while washing waves over the deck. Two men on the other ship were bailing out water while a couple of others wheeled a large slingshot onto the deck. The boat rocked so much that the thing rolled from side to side, once colliding with the railing.

"Do they intend to attack us?" Perrin asked.

Verbena replied, "Maybe, but they're too far away for that thing to be of any use."

The men on the deck secured the apparatus to the mast and loaded it, anyway.

Then another brought an object that looked like a keg and placed it in the sling. He released the chain... and the object flew in the air far short of where Captain Anko's boat lay.

What were they doing?

But then a shockwave went through the water. And a wave bulged up and bulged and bulged until the dome of water split. A great spout of water whooshed into the air. Drops fell back to the surface like heavy rain. Perrin could feel the wet spray on the skin of his arms.

Then it went quiet.

On the other ship, a line of people stood on the deck and peered over the water.

"They used an underwater explosive to chase off the whales," Captain Anko said.

"Why?"

"Same as us: they want to get through, so they scared off the whales."

"Is that going to work?"

"Not for long. What's worse is they'll bring the entire army of whales on them and we'll be stuck here with them."

Not only that, they had a dragon that the whales professed to object to passing through their land.

"It's time we had a proper discussion with these whales," Perrin said.

Captain Anko turned to him. "Didn't you just do that?"

"I tried, but it's really hard to hear and keep the trumpet under water, and you can't see properly either. They seem to refuse to talk to us, but I can't understand why."

"That's the ocean for you. Any ideas on how to fix that?"

"Yes, I might have an idea."

CHAPTER 23

There was no time to lose, but when Perrin explained what he had in mind, Captain Anko's eyes widened. He burst out, "Do you know how much those bells are worth? They're not mine either. Until I deliver them, they are the property of the Foundry and they would be very upset if something happened. Not to mention charge me a substantial amount of money."

"You have a crane on board to lift cargo to the quay, yes?"

"Of course. What else is a crane for?"

"You trust your crane to be safe and stable and not to drop the cargo on your ship or on the quay or into the water?"

"Of course!"

"Then what is the difference between unloading the cargo and suspending it on the surface to allow me to talk to the whales?"

"We're in the middle of the ocean!"

"Yes, but the weather is calm. I'm only asking you to hang one bell in the water so I can sit inside and converse better with the whales. Because they don't understand that I come to bring back their treasure. I need to make that clear to them."

Hix snorted. "Hmph, I say we turn around while we still can and forget about this treasure. They don't like the dragon. How about we get rid of it first?"

The dragon had been fairly quiet through all of this, mostly sitting on the deck on her nest of empty eggs. Perrin didn't know how long she would stay that calm, or whether the male might turn up again.

"That would take a lot of time we don't have. We're here now. Let me talk to the whales. We might stop that other ship from doing something stupid."

But the most stupid thing the other ship could do was to board the *Seven Seas* with force and demand the trumpet—which they had probably come to do anyway—and Perrin wanted to be rid of the thing before he had to grapple with pumans and their lackeys, because he held no illusions about his or the crew's ability to fend off giant cats, no matter how big and strong Quinn was.

The thought of the other ship "doing something stupid" swayed Captain Anko, who probably didn't like the thought of having to turn around either, so he instructed Hix to help Perrin.

The large bells stood on the deck.

Seawater would not be very good for the metal, but he guessed they could oil them and clean them thoroughly once they were out of the water.

While Hix set up the crane, Perrin and Verbena went to look in the cargo compartment of the ship to see if there was anything else he could use.

Most of the cargo consisted of crates full of boxes and goods in parcels that were all wrapped up neatly.

"What sort of thing are you looking for?" Verbena asked.

"Mainly something that will allow me to see underwater

better than that viewing tube that only gives me a tiny window to look through."

He wormed himself in between the boxes and opened some that contained different types of tiles in different colours. Those boxes were too heavy to shift, so he couldn't look in the ones underneath.

Next he found bags with dried beans and a box that contains jars of *Grandma Sookie's Raspberry Jam*. He knew Grandma Sookie. She had a stall at the markets, but he had no idea she exported her jams. They were very nice, he had to admit.

"You mean, something like this?" Verbena said.

She stood in the next narrow walkway and held aloft a large glass bowl. It was bigger than her head and shaped like a ball with a hole in one end.

Perrin knew these things. Some people used them to keep pet mice or frogs. One would put straw in the bottom, or rocks and a layer of water.

But this thing was perfect for what he wanted. "Yes, exactly like that!"

Perrin then got dressed in his red and white bathing suit, because he suspected that he was going to get wet, and because it would be hot inside the bell. Up on the deck, Hix had opened the crate that contained the largest of the bells, and the crane was in position. Ivy was attaching the chain and ropes to the little knobs on the top and the wooden frame underneath.

The dragon was looking at all these activities without doing anything.

Perrin went to help.

He forced himself to ignore sniggers and stares from the crew. Yes, the suit was ridiculous. His pale hairy legs didn't help either.

The idea was that he would climb onto the wooden beams and the bell would be lowered over the side with him inside it.

Once the bell was in the water, a hose would pump air into the space underneath so that he could continue to breathe but also that he could better communicate with the whales.

Perrin eyed the structure.

Yes, he would get very wet, even if Hix had attached a basket to the structure for him to sit on.

Perrin had his trumpet and glass bowl ready.

In the distance, he could see the passage where the whales circled. Occasionally, they would lift their heads out of the water and look on, but would never come closer.

Even while the ocean was relatively calm, lifting the bell out of the crate was a delicate operation that took much longer than Perrin liked. This was not helped by the fact that there was a dragon on the deck who became mildly alarmed at the machinery reaching overhead.

Perrin kept looking at the other ship, but they had anchored in a bay on the other side of the passage, near the other island, and there was no one to be seen on board.

Pumans liked to be active at night, Perrin remembered uncomfortably.

Except no one had seen any pumans yet and the other ship was yet to acknowledge the *Seven Seas* and its crew.

Once the bell hung over the side, the ship listed badly, and the waves would wash over the deck. Quinn had to help Perrin climb into it from the railing.

He settled on the basket and took the bowl from Quinn, who reached up from underneath. Next came the hose. Ivy stood at the pump that would provide him with air. He tied the hose to the frame and gave the thumbs up.

Then the bell went down. It hit the surface and water entered around his feet. The water was cold, and it was so dark in here.

He knocked on the metal. Twice, which meant all was fine.

Now he'd best hurry up. It was quite stuffy under the bell

already, and this was an odd combination with the cold water that washed over his feet.

He put the bell of the trumpet into the water and blew into it. Then while still holding the trumpet, he manoeuvred the viewing bowl into place.

Yes, this was much better than the captain's viewing tube.

With that device, on the surface in the dinghy, he had only been able to see the murky darkness, but now he could make out lighter patches of sand and darker rocks on the bottom.

Gradually, as his eyes got increasingly used to the low light, he could start to make out other things. Seaweed attached to the rocks waved gently in the current. Schools of little silver fish darted between the fronds. Anemones with white tentacles crowded on a rocky knoll. A grey fish with red stripes about the length of his arm swam lazily over a seagrass bed.

Then suddenly there was panic. The large fish scooted into the seaweed.

A tail came into vision.

A very large tail.

It slid away and was replaced by a barnacle-encrusted back with a big chunky fin.

The whale swam past. Perrin bobbed in his enclosure.

He put the bell of the trumpet in the water and shouted through it, "I can see you down there. I am here to listen. I have the Horn of Truth to return to you, but I want passage to Solania in return."

A series of garbled sound came through the trumpet. The whales were very, very close, even if he couldn't see them. Perrin could feel the water moving as they passed.

Then one of the creatures, a whale that looked old and was covered in barnacles, hovered under the bell. Its eye was very close to the glass bowl.

It let out a squeal that made the bell ring so much that Perrin's ears hurt.

"We told you to go away," the trumpet translated. "After what you did to us yesterday, we have nothing more to say."

Perrin shouted. "We have nothing to do with the other ship. We're happy to travel peacefully."

"But yet you do. They came because of you. They chase us off because they know what you're doing here."

"Yes, that's why I'm returning the Horn of Truth to you."

"Why can't you understand that there is no Horn of Truth?"

"What do you mean? I'm holding it."

"You may call it such, but the Horn of Truth is not a true Gaminian legend."

"How can you say this? We've come this way to return it, because people in our town were willing to commit crimes to obtain it and because the owners received a screamer demanding for it to be returned."

"We did not send it. We're not the only folk to use screamers. In fact, we rarely use them these days. There is no Horn of Truth. There are devices, like the one you hold, that have the power to translate your garbled noises into speech we can understand, but there are many such. There is no one device that lends special power. A metalsmith in Validor makes these for us, and if the king deems it necessary, he orders an extra specimen to be made. Sadly, nothing you land folk make holds a natural beauty, so it takes a while for the instrument to acquire a remotely agreeable appearance, which also doesn't last outside the confines of the ocean. You're holding one of the instruments, yes. But it's by far not the only one and it holds no special meaning."

"Do you mean..."

"It means that it looks like you've been conned."

"But who would do that?"

"That is not our problem."

Perrin's head reeled. It was also getting quite hot and stuffy inside the bell, despite the fresh air still bubbling in through the hose every time Ivy operated the pump. There was not enough fresh air coming in. Maybe Ivy was getting tired. He would have to get out soon.

But still, he found it very hard to believe what the whale said, and that he had really come here—and Roban's business had been broken into—for nothing.

"What about all the old books that tell us about this treasure? They can't be all wrong."

"Those books were written by wizards who had an interest in people believing that there was only one device, because then, any they laid their hands on became valuable so they could sell it to gullible people."

It all made far too much sense. After he had seen the dregs of the collection in Atreyo's family's house, and heard the history of it from Sabyna. Wizards tricking common people into parting with money was a very common theme running through crime cases in Tamba. Perrin could now hit himself over the head for letting himself be taken in by one such story.

But he still found it hard to believe.

"Is there not even an original Horn of Truth that is the source of the legend?"

"Legends are things of land folk. We don't bother ourselves with silly stories and beliefs. We see the things as they *are*. Your trinkets have value for us when they are useful, but they do not have a value beyond their use. I cannot tell you why you land folk believe otherwise."

All right. This was leading nowhere.

It had now gotten so stuffy inside the bell that Perrin seriously had to think about getting out.

But if the whales didn't want the trumpet back, then what

was he supposed to do with it and who had been sending these threatening messages to Roban and his family?

"Can we at least be granted passage to Solania?"

"Not while you have that creature on board. We have already told you that. The king's decision about this is final."

"We have a travel permit. I can show it to you."

"You said nothing about carrying this creature across our land."

"The dragon will stay safely on the deck of the ship."

"You will not bring this beast across our land. We will stop you, sink your vessel, and keep your souls hostage for eternity. That is our final word."

There was no point in discussing any further. Besides, a lot of whales had joined and were swimming around underneath the bell.

Strange sounds reverberated through the water, as if something was happening elsewhere.

He knocked on the wall of the bell. Three times, the sign that he wanted to be pulled up. A muffled ringing tone sounded through the water.

A moment later, the bell was being pulled up and not much later, it cleared the surface of the water. The air that came in was fresh and beautiful, but the sounds that drifted in worried him. Shouts and bangs.

The bell moved low over the water and then over the railing onto the desk. Perrin climbed out first, wet, shivering and blinded by the abundance of light.

But then he saw it: in the time he'd been under water, the other boat had come close and people on the deck were throwing grappling hooks to catch the railing of the *Seven Seas*. Some of those people were normal men, but others were pumans.

CHAPTER 24

There was no time for Perrin to tell Captain Anko about the bad news he had learned from the whales.

The pumans were about to come on board.

The captain himself stood at the railing brandishing a sword.

Three of the grappling hooks had caught onto the railing on the side of the deck where the dragon sat.

She was agitated, standing over the nest with her wings spread, crouching low as if to spring.

Ivy and Verbena were trying to disengage the grappling hooks from the railing with the deck's broom, but they couldn't quite reach.

After setting the bell down on the deck, Hix joined the captain at the railing.

Verbena pulled off one of her long socks, put a lead weight in the bottom and slung this around the rope. She yanked before the sock could unwind itself. The rope and hook fell into the water.

Ivy cheered. Hix slashed at another rope, but it proved hard to cut. Verbena tried to do the same with that rope, but it was under too much strain.

The pumans on the other deck pulled and pulled. The rope strained. When Verbena's sock couldn't dislodge the hook, Hix slashed at the rope with a knife. But the ships were unstoppably drifting together.

The people and pumans on board stood ready to jump. They wore leather armour and held weapons.

Perrin grabbed the nearest weapon he could find, which was a metal bucket. He was highly tempted to toss the trumpet into the bucket and fling it at the other ship, since the whales told him it had no value to them.

But on the other hand, it had value for *someone* even if it wasn't the whales, and someone had considered it valuable enough to send this team of miscreants to retrieve it.

And Perrin was highly reluctant to give in before he knew what he was giving up. The possibility crossed his mind that trapping him here, out in the ocean where he could disappear without a trace, was all part of the plan.

Was Roban part of the plan?

And Mirella?

Had they tricked him into helping so that they could get rid of him? Why? They'd won their share of Atreyo's money in the court case. What more did they want?

His mind whirled while he watched the ships come closer together.

He knew one thing: he would not give up without a fight.

As the ship came closer and closer, he became aware of a noise from behind the other ship. The ocean frothed with movement of thousands of fish and white foam.

A giant head stuck out of the water, belonging to a whale much bigger than he'd ever seen.

Someone yelled. A couple of pumans abandoned their positions facing Captain Anko and the crew of the *Seven Seas*.

They ran across the deck of their ship to help a mate load the cannon that pointed in the other direction.

A whale raised its head and upper body out of the water. It fell and slapped the surface so hard that the spray of water fell over both ships.

Perrin wiped the salt from his face.

The pumans shouted. One of the men had lost his footing and almost washed overboard with the water.

His mate managed to load the projectile into the cannon and another lit the fuse.

Perrin clamped his hands over his ears.

Boom.

The projectile flew over the ocean and landed in the sea.

A moment later, a deep rumble sounded, the water bulged up, exploded and sprayed all over the two boats. The whales retreated. The pumans on the deck of the other boat cheered.

Meanwhile, their mates at the ropes pulled and pulled until the two boats came together. Perrin grabbed his bucket.

The first puman jumped the distance between the boats.

"Keep off my boat, you scum!" Captain Anko yelled. He swung his shortsword, but even to Perrin, it was clear that he had little fighting experience.

But the crew had even less. Hix and Quinn made a valiant effort, armed with sticks and brooms. Ivy held a net.

But Verbena had pressed herself against the wall of the captain's cabin, her face white.

"I don't know what to do!" she shouted when Perrin looked in her direction. "I don't know anything about fighting! My sister tells me to keep away if there is a fight!"

Perrin started, "Maybe you could—"

But he stopped when an almighty roar cut through the panic and noise.

Perrin turned around.

The red male dragon had returned.

He flew low over the ships. He was much bigger than the female, who still sat under the mast with the nest, holding out her wings.

She looked, for all Perrin could see, frightened. She held her head low to the deck, crouching over her eggs.

The pumans had been about to come on board, but now they fled across the deck.

The dragon went after them, landing on the other boat with a thud, making both ships rock violently. The hulls clonked against each other.

One of the pumans yelled. The dragon swiped him aside with his claw. He slid across the deck, into the water. The whales had returned there, and this time they had brought some help from black and white killer whales. Perrin wasn't keen to watch what happened on that side of the ship.

"All attack!" the puman captain yelled.

He jumped from his boat to the deck of the *Seven Seas*.

The other pumans jumped, too, still looking menacing, even if it seemed to be that they were trying to get away from the dragon.

The other ship had at least ten crew members on board, pumans and men. Captain Anko and his crew were outnumbered. They did the best they could, but they were not fighters.

Captain Anko slashed with his shortsword at anyone who came within reach. Quinn hit a man overboard with his broom.

Cats hated water. He went down with a squeal. A back fin from a killer whale came into view and disappeared again.

Ivy threw the net and managed to pull a puman into the

water. Even Verbena swung her sock with the lead weights inside. She knocked out an attacker in this manner.

But other pumans made it on board. They were strong and fast. One of them climbed into the mast.

"Get him down!" Hix yelled.

The male dragon hissed from the other boat.

The other pumans ran along the tiny strip of deck outside of the railing of the *Seven Seas*. They ran past the captain's cabin and the remains of the dragon's crate, onto the deck.

Perrin couldn't see what happened there, but a loud yell and a roar gave him some indication. The female dragon objected.

Perrin yelled at Verbena, "Come on, help me!"

She abandoned her sock-swinging and stepped into his linked hands to climb onto the roof of the cabin. Then she helped him up.

From the roof, they could survey the entire scene.

The deck was a mess. The dragon had pulled everything it could get loose into the nest at the bottom of the mast. It had also clawed deep gauges into the deck and the crates of cargo that still stood there.

The male dragon perched on the railing of the other ship.

Two pumans ran past—straight at the dragon defending her nest.

The dragon sprang forward, but she was still attached to the heavy base of the crate and couldn't quite reach the men, but they were scared enough that they ran back again.

Captain Anko waited for them with his sword at the entrance to his cabin. They avoided his sword.

The boat rocked violently as something hit it from underneath. This was followed by the splash of a massive tail on the surface.

The female dragon then turned to the male. She roared at him. Just as well that she was still attached to the base of the crate, or she would have jumped to the other boat. Now she yanked at the rope.

The boat rocked, and the mast swung like crazy.

The puman in the mast hung on for dear life. He was slowly letting himself down, no doubt afraid he would lose his grip.

Perrin had an idea. First, he swung the tip of the loading crane away from the mast and locked it into position so that not even a cat-like puman could jump the distance between the two.

Then he lowered himself from the roof onto the deck of the ship. Verbena watched with wide eyes.

He snuck along the outside of the railing, avoiding looking at the churning water down there and the large shapes that passed under the boat. He approached the dragon's nest from behind.

While the dragon was occupied at the railing, snarling at the male dragon, he used the broom to push the cloths of nest all around the mast so that the puman who was now forced to come all the way down the mast could not avoid stepping in it. There were nineteen eggs. They were soft and rubbery and although Perrin knew they could not contain any young, he could not bring himself to damage them.

When it was done, he ran away again to the safe side of the deck.

Captain Anko was still fighting at the rear deck. Quinn and Ivy had joined in. Hix had located an ancient pistol and was trying to get a clean shot of two men hiding behind a crate.

With a roar, the male dragon jumped to the ship. Verbena gave a squeal. She rolled aside and dropped from the roof of the cabin just before the creature landed there. The ship rocked. A gush of water came over the deck. The wooden cabin creaked in protest under the sheer weight of the creature. It was huge. The claws of a foot curved over the edge of the roof. Those claws would rip a person apart.

A puman with a crossbow ran from the fight at the rear deck.

He loosed an arrow which simply bounced off the armoured plates on the dragon's chest. The dragon lashed out with its tail and knocked the man off his feet.

While he fell over the edge of the roof onto the deck, another puman put an arrow to his bow, but when the arrow hit the dragon straight in the head, it glanced off and fell into the water.

The dragon jumped onto the deck and advanced slowly to the female, swinging his tail.

The female retreated, just as the remaining puman had come down the mast and stood in the nest.

She let out a roar and, in one massive jump, crossed to the mast. She grabbed the puman in her jaws and shook him like a dog.

The puman squealed.

The dragon threw the puman onto the deck with a heavy thud. He did not get up. The male dragon arched his neck. Perrin had heard the rumbling sound it made before.

The hiss of spewing fire rent the air as he ran and ducked behind the cabin. He found Quinn, Ivy and Verbena already there.

Then the boat rocked violently again.

"They've jumped to the pirate ship," Captain Anko said.

Perrin peeked around the corner of the cabin. The rope that had restrained the female dragon lay burned and broken on the deck. Both dragons were on the deck of the puman ship. They hissed flames, they hit overboard anyone who came out on the deck.

"What are they doing?" Ivy asked.

"They're killing all the pumans," her brother said.

"We better make sure we're not next," Perrin said.

"No," Captain Anko said. He still held his sword. His shirt was torn and one of his sleeves was wet with blood.

"Those beasts!" He panted. "They're helping us."

It was true.

The fire on board had spread. Two more pirates jumped from the deck into the reach of the killer whales.

Captain Anko yelled, "Now!"

The crew ran forward to disengage the grappling hooks from the railing.

They stood on the deck and watched. They watched as the distance between the ships became larger. As the two dragons tore the ship apart and set fire to the cabin and then, as the female lifted her tail and doused the deck with a backwards spray of stinking urine. This was clearly a sign to the male. He tried to approach her, his male tackle ready for action, but she was having none of it. She sprang at him, grabbing him by the throat, scratching and hissing fire. He pushed her flat on her belly onto the deck. Blood ran from several scratches on his neck and front paws. Her head lay flat on the deck, her nostrils breathing smoke and her eyes wide open. The expression of anger in them shocked Perrin.

Just as the male dragon was shuffling to get into position, she raised herself, and tipped him off the side into the water. A dragon in the water was like a bat on the land: awkward and vulnerable. After a struggle where Perrin wondered if he'd get out at all, the dragon managed to get the wind in his wings, and flew off.

By this time, the pirate ship was clearly sinking. The female dragon flew low over the water, landed at her nest, and started licking the scratches she had sustained in the process. She looked exhausted.

The puman ship drifted away, burning, sinking, floating helplessly through the waves.

The male dragon circled high overhead.

Then Quinn yelled, "look!"

A huge whale had appeared at the surface, an ancient animal that looked older than time itself.

Perrin was almost certain that this was the whale king.

Oh no, would they now have to fight the whales. He had no energy left. He didn't think the crew was in a better shape.

But the whale just watched.

After a while, the whale jerked his head ever so slightly upwards and made a long wailing sound.

"What does that mean?" Verbena asked.

"He wants us to follow him," Captain Anko said.

Follow a whale into a watery grave?

CHAPTER 25

The crew debated briefly amongst themselves about what to do now. Both Captain Anko and Hix remained adamant that the whale's behaviour meant that they were to follow. They'd travelled to Gaminia before. They brushed aside Quinn's fears. Yes, whales were big and they could be angry, but the best way to avoid angry whales was to do as they asked.

Yes, they still had the dragon, but she was spent and bleeding and had curled up under the mast.

So they followed.

The whales came from everywhere to the waters surrounding the boat. Their bodies all pointed in the direction of the channel that led into Gaminia.

A few smooth black killer whales lined up next to the ship. One of them even nudged the hull.

It was true, the whales were guiding the ship through the passage.

In the distance the puman ship still floated, now a burnt-out husk of its former incarnation. Those bandits were not going to be an issue anymore.

More and more whales accompanied the ship, their puffs of breath rising up everywhere. The giant whale Perrin judged to be the whale king continued to swim next to the *Seven Seas*. Captain Anko made sure that the crew kept the ship at a distance.

Perrin climbed down the ladder so he could stick the trumpet in the water.

"What's going on? Why are you letting us through now?"

The large whale's deep voice replied, "You stopped the robbers."

"The pumans?"

A loud angry squeal made Perrin jump. "Those folk are not worthy to be named. Those who stop the evil folk of thieves and robbers can pass our lands."

"Even a dragon?"

"Just this once, to bring the creature home. We won't let any further creatures through."

"I have no intention of going sailing with a dragon again. What about the trumpet? Are you sure you don't want it?"

"Keep it in your place of authority. It may be useful in the future. You and your companions are free to use it to appeal to our kingdom. If you use it, we will reply."

Well, that was something Inspector Carbin would be happy with. The Bureau was sure to intercept other items that belonged to Gaminia.

The whale king continued, "Do be careful, because these won't have been the only sharks who seek to enrich themselves through the value attributed to our artefacts. Listen: this is the only truth. The whales do not value possessions, and anyone who tells you otherwise is at best lying or at worst, trying to gain an advantage at your expense."

After that conversation, Perrin put the trumpet back into its case, still wondering who had set the pumans up to go after it and why.

But from his time with Atreyo, he knew that rich collectors of artefacts were strange people who did strange things for reasons that no one, including the sellers of those items, understood.

In private, Atreyo would have smiled at him and said, *Why stand in between a fool and his mad rush to spend money?*

And Perrin would have laughed.

But now he felt uneasy. Things were rarely as simple as that. He made a promise to himself. He'd look after the trumpet and make sure it was well-guarded at the Bureau.

For most of the rest of the day and night and the next day, the ship glided through Gaminia, accompanied by its huge guard of whales. Perrin collected his glass bowl from his cabin and watched the scene underneath the ship. There were so many whales!

They floated past large seaweed beds and meadows of seagrass, large schools of small fish and rocky outcrops with anemones, more fish and big fat shells. They were things he only knew from the markets.

Seals darted around the rocky cliffs, occasionally sticking their heads above the water to look at the passing ship.

The dragon lay on the deck with her head over the side, also looking at the abundance of animals passing underneath. She did not growl or breathe fire, but only watched.

Once they passed the island group, they were out in open water again.

From there on, it was only a short trip to Solania and its capital of Seahaven. Perrin had been here before, when he travelled with Atreyo.

He found that things were different when he was in charge of his own expedition. And also when he had to apply for entry into the harbour of the dragon. He couldn't enjoy the sight of the crowded little houses around the harbour, but had to meet with harbour officials before mooring. He had to make assurances that the dragon posed no danger—he could do no such thing, so he requested the assistance of a magician or dragon handler instead.

The agreed dragon handler came to the ship to prepare the creature. He looked like a typical wizard with a beard and a blue cloak. Only his beard was black rather than grey.

The man was astonished at the sight of the nest and even more astonished that she had been able to fend off a male.

"Those are good dragons," the man said. "They're the dragons that go to the grandwizard's palace."

That palace stuck out over the tops of the roofs of the town, looming over Solania's citizenry.

The *Seven Seas* was allowed to shore.

People from the palace came on board to collect the dragon, wearing fire-proof suits and carrying ropes and giant cattle prods.

They brought a new crate and pushed and prodded the dragon into it. She was protective of the eggs, but, not being fertilised, they were weak and two had already broken and released foul-smelling slime onto the deck.

In the end, the dragon handlers shoved the lot into the crate and shut the door.

That looked very unsophisticated and not at all what he expected to happen in a magical place.

In all, Perrin almost felt sorry to part with the dragon. The dragon had been an important part of this year of his life.

While the harbour workers were loading the creature onto another boat to be taken inland, Perrin became aware of a commotion on the quayside.

A group of brightly dressed people was coming towards him. At the front was a tall man with a long grey beard wearing a white robe. Perrin recognised this man from a previous trip: Grandmaster Yorick.

The party stopped at the bottom of the gangplank, and the grandmaster slowly climbed onto the deck. He studied Perrin up and down.

"So, I seem to remember you," Grandmaster Yorick said when he stood next to Perrin. "Aren't you the annoying pen pusher who insists to want to return dragons to Solania, as if we are waiting for more dragons. And before that, you were always complaining about the books."

"Because they were never right, and I could prove it."

"Hmph. It seems you finally have your way, but that's not why I'm here."

"No?"

Perrin hadn't expected the grandmaster to turn up personally, anyway.

"No. It seems you have something that belongs to us, that you've had some trouble with and we'd gladly take off your hands in return for not bothering you and asking any more questions about the dragon."

Perrin's mouth almost fell open. So it was the Solanians all along, trying to make out that the trumpet was valuable and sending the pumans after it.

"Do we?" Perrin said. He looked at the crew. Captain Anko gave him a tiny nod. "I don't know what you're talking about. We did have a thing that needed to be returned to Gaminia, but we returned it to Gaminia and don't have it anymore."

A puzzled look came over the grandwizard's face. "Really? What sort of thing was this?"

"Oh, just a rusty old trumpet full of barnacles. Someone in town received a screamer from Gamina that demanded it to be returned to the whales. So we returned it to them. Well, I did, after I convinced the owner to give it to me."

"Oh." An expression of uncomfortable comprehension came over his face. He repeated, "Oh." And then, "Well, that ended in a fine manner, then."

"Yes, it certainly did."

The grandmaster turned around and walked with his entourage along the harbourfront.

Perrin and Verbena could barely contain their laughter until he was out of earshot.

About the Author

Patty Jansen lives in Sydney, Australia, where she spends most of her time writing Science Fiction and Fantasy.

Her career started in earnest when her story *This Peaceful State of War* placed first in the second quarter of the Writers of the Future contest and was published in their 27th anthology. She has also sold fiction to genre magazines such as Analog Science Fiction and Fact, Redstone SF and Aurealis, before making the move to independent publishing.

Patty has written over fifty novels in both Science Fiction and Fantasy, including the *Icefire Trilogy* and the *Ambassador* series.

pattyjansen.com

BOOKS BY PATTY JANSEN

MORE INFORMATION:

PATTYJANSEN.COM

For a complete list of books, scan the image below with your phone.

9 781925 841244